The Vice President

Written

By

Elina Salajeva

'A Powerful Suspenseful Tale of
Power and Murder,'

'Until the End, You Will Never Know
Who to Trust,'

The Vice President

DISCLAIMER

This is a work of fiction. Names, characters, businesses, places, events, and incidents are either the products of the author's imagination or used in a fictitious manner. Any resemblance to actual persons, living or dead, or actual events is purely coincidental.

DEDICATION

Riches and Prosperity.

TABLE OF CONTENTS

ACKNOWLEDGMENTS

A big thanks to Touchladybirdlucky
Studios.

The Vice President

Elina Salajeva

CHAPTER ONE

A beautiful blonde girl is sitting on the stairs with her legs stretched wearing rare white jean trousers and a big coat that seems to mop the dust from the stairs. The big coat is spread all over the stairs. She is wearing high heel stilettos of badge color. It's not the clothes that drew the attention, no. It's the look on her face. Red-colored small lips and staring deep blue eyes. Her hair is twisted and overhanging forward nearly covering her right eye. Both her hands are touching the floor. She looked exhausted or shocked by something. She had been sat there for some time now. It's the noise of high heel shoes that startled her. She seemed to have been in a trance of some sort, her mind very far away in a world of her own. Red high heel shoes stepped down the stairs. A woman in her mid-twenties walked down the stairs wearing a matching short, lovely red dress with no arms and one that revealed half her chest. She is holding a glass of wine in her hand. She puts a handkerchief on the stairs next to the blonde girl and sits next to her. She sips her wine and sighs. A moment passed by without anyone saying anything.

"That's life, what can you do," said Jacqueline.

"I still can't believe this actually happened and somehow, I can't stop thinking about it," added Valentine.

Augustin ran away heading toward the main house shouting his sister's name.

Under the garden shade, an old man is sitting on the swing wooden bench. He swung forward and backward. He looked further down and smiled. It's now just a dream. He recalled that at one point he was the most important and busiest man in the town. He had people coming to him every day, to pick his brain. He is a shadow of the man he was. Over the years no one seemed bothered about him. Days had gone by without even a single person coming to him for any advice or information.

Augustin ran toward the swing bench. When he was about to sit on the bench Wendy pushed him off. He fell to the ground and bruised his leg.

"Wendy stop pushing your brother away. There is enough space for all of us why push your brother away?" asked grandpa.

"He is a bully; he is hiding my doll."

"Grandpa, she broke my van, the one dad bought for me."

"It was by accident after all that was a stupid van. I would not play with a van that carries dead people," said Wendy.

"I don't care if it carries dead people or not it was mine you had no right to break it."

"Stupid. How many times did I tell you that it was an accident? I sat in your van by accident. You can't compare my doll to that stupid van. Every day you break my van, you break my van. Keep on making noise about that stupid van and maybe I will end up breaking you too."

"I don't understand why you fight that much. Let's sit together. I will tell you a great story," said grandpa.

Augustin and Wendy jumped onto the swing bench and waited eagerly to hear the grandpa's story.

In the big city, Alfred is in office buildings. He is a young man full of beans and promises. He had just been given his new job in the treasury department. He entered the conference room. A big room with two flat screens in front, a big desk with a telecommunication system at one end. He sat down and opened his laptop. He went through the screens before he heard a knock on the door and before he answered, a man dressed to kill opened the door.

Peeped in and entered the room.

"Hello Sir, thanks for coming at such short notice but there is something I think you should see," said Alfred.

"Better be important you know how busy I am," replied Bernard.

Bernard had been in his job for over twenty years now.

He knew this kid might have unraveled something big. In his late forties, always well-dressed with a clean shave. He was a bit overweight with a big belly hanging, hence the use of cross belts all the time. He wore expensive shoes. He remembered the first days he started his job. Alfred was a mirror of himself years back.

"So, what is it young Alfred?" asked Bernard.

"Sir, look at this," said Alfred walking to the two big screens in front. He is holding a stick in his hand. He arrived a few feet from the screens and looked at Bernard who stood next to him.

"Yes, go on."

"I looked at the data for the last 5 years. Look at this graph. In fact, total spending has been increasing at an alarming rate. Look at the other screen. Look at the budget proposals and the actual figures," said Alfred.

Bernard looked at the screens one at a time.

"Well spotted young Alfred. Can you look at the figures for the past ten and twenty years and let me know the results before the end of the week? I also want that report on my desk by the end of the day. Good job well done," said Bernard leaving the conference room.

The young Alfred smiles and remained standing at the two big screens. What really was going on?

Bernard entered a beautiful big office. It has brown wooden cabinets. It has a big desk with an ivory decorated comfy sofa with white cushions. In front, it has two other comfy sofas with a small table with a drawer. Above these two chairs is a big mirror on the ceiling. To the right is a big window with eight small panels. Bernard sits down and picks up the phone.

"Hello, Senator I think there is something you should see. When is the perfect time and place to meet and talk about this? Your office should I say?" asked Bernard.

"Yes. My office later today or meet at the launch of the same place? Your call?" replied Senator Brice.

"This can't wait, meet you at your office in the afternoon," replied Bernard.

Later that day, Bernard arrived at the Senator's office in the heart of the city. This was a flamboyant government building where all important government officials had their offices hence the tight security. Bernard passed through security and went over all security checks despite being known as an important member of the government. He had been here several times. He and the Senator goes back a long way. They had gone to university together. The Senator, a charming man. With him what you see is what you get because of this he soon finds himself loved by many and hated by many as well, whereas Bernard with his sweet-talking laid back approach finds himself in the government offices downtown. There is a thin line between success and failure in politics. Sometimes it's all just luck but in most cases, the saying that fortune favors the brave has some truth in it.

Bernard entered the office blocks leading to the Senator's office. He opened the door and saw the Senator in the corridor talking to one of the advisers.

"Senator," said Bernard stretching his hand.

"Yes, Bernard. Please come on in," replied the Senator stretching his hand showing Bernard the way.

The Senator's adviser soon disappears, and the two men entered the office. The big wooden door is slammed behind them.

"My friend, what brings you here. Yeah, just like the old days. But the better man won, huh? You must agree. I always told you to take the bull by its horns. Politics is a dirty game too. They say if you want to die with a bullet in your chest become a politician," said the Senator.

He paused before he continued talking.

"So how have you been, Bernard?"

"Good, nice to see you. Been sometime. Busy all the time. Problems everywhere we can't even have time to sit down together."

"I know. You know what? Bring Emmy to my house for dinner this weekend. Say Saturday night.

"Will certainly do Brice," replied Bernard.

"So, what brings you here? You said you have something to show me?"

"Yes, Senator. Look at these figures for the past five years," said Bernard handing over the file to the Senator.

The Senator looked at the file for a while.

He stood up and walked to the big window.

"So, what is your explanation for all this?"

"Someone is embezzling some funds from the treasury. I think this has been going on for some time now," said Bernard.

The Senator walked back and sat in his comfy sofa.

"How can one do that unnoticed? Our system is robust and is regularly checked. Stealing, I doubt that."

"It's possible. One can create ghost accounts. The rate is alarming. Every system has its shock waves to offset the rapid rise. But for the past few years, the trend has been enormous."

"Okay. You have a point. I will meet with the Vice President and ask her if we can establish a task force to look at this."

CHAPTER TWO

Susanne and Sydney are a very happy couple blessed with twin girls. They have a huge house in the suburbs, and they have worked very hard to give their daughters a good life.

"The girls are all grown up now, soon they will be moving out of the house. Don't you think maybe after that we should sell this big house and buy a smaller house maybe go on vacation with the sale proceeds," asked Sydney.

"Darling what got into you. This is not just a house. There are memories attached to this house. This is our home. What got into you to even suggest something like that? We are not selling this house. I want all my daughters one day to bring all their kids here," replied Susanne.

Rosemarie and Roselyn are in their bedroom talking to each other. Roselyn is sitting down cuddling a big teddy bear. She looked worried. Her right chin is in contact with the teddy bear. Rosemary is standing facing the mirror. She is putting makeup on her face. Occasionally she looks back to make eye contact with her sister.

"You seemed worried about something lately. What is it?" asked Rosemary.

"We have grown up now, and the clock is not stopping for anyone. I am just worried about leaving the house. Mum and dad and you might end up leaving me too," said Roselyn.

"Don't be silly I will always be there for you. We will always be together. We can always visit mum and dad."

"Yes, but what if you get married and probably your husband won't like it when we are always together?"

"Okay, how about we find twins too as boyfriends so that it will be easy. That way we can do everything together. We can all stay together," replied Rosemary.

Roselyn raised her head and placed the teddy bear aside with a big smile on her face.

"You will do that for me? For us? Oh, thank you, sister. Imagine all of us visiting mum and dad that should be bliss."

"Yes, Roselyn but first we must get a good job or career. We will need a big place to stay together."

Roselyn sat down and clutched her teddy bear. While Rosemary does her hair and lips before looking through the mirror at her twin sister.

"What is it now? I thought we discussed all your worries?"

"Rosemary, are you not afraid to die? As we grow up, we get closer to death as well you know? Especially in our case, we might all die together."

"What's wrong with you today. We will die when we are very old. Yes, there are chances we might die one after the other but hey everyone dies. We are all going to die. It's not a big issue."

"I read in the papers a few weeks ago, that twins in Russia both died at the same time one after the other," said Roselyn.

"Were they old? How did they die?" asked Rosemary.

"They were very young in their late thirties. One was involved in a car accident."

"Do you mean they were both involved in the accident?"

"No, Rosemary, only one was involved in a car accident. The other one was miles away but when he received the news of the death of his twin brother, he died as well."

"What? You might have misread the paper. When was this? Are you sure? I never heard anything like that before," said Rosemary.

"Ever since I read this article, I have been worrying for you, for us?"

"Listen, Roselyn, if I die whether from a natural cause or an accident it doesn't necessarily mean you will die too. You can live up to a hundred years more on your own. All this is just a coincidence. Let me check the article," said Rosemary. Rosemary and Roselyn surrounded the laptop on the desk in their bedroom. Rosemary researched the article. Minutes later they found the article.

"Hey. You are right. That's a bit odd I think."

"Rosemary, can you see if you can find the autopsy reports of the twins?"

The ladies searched for the autopsy reports, but they were not available. The closest information they got was reported by closer relatives. The first twin was involved in a car accident. He never stood a chance. Death was instant. The other twin died after hearing the death of his twin. He died from shock. As far as they know he was in perfect health.

"Sis, now you see why I got worried," asked Roselyn.

Rosemary just nodded her head, she sits next to her sister, and they hugged each other.

Vladivostok is sunny and beautiful. Everyone is busy as usual with their day-to-day chores. The port is busy with boats coming and going. Vladivostok is a port near the border with North Korea and China. Loren a woman of Chinese origin in her late years is in the coffee shop. She sips her tea and looked outside the window. She can see the boats lined up outside on the port. Since she has been in the coffee shop more than five boats have arrived. She recalled the last time she was here many years ago, not much has changed since then.

"Do you want more coffee? It seems your cup is now empty?" asked the coffee shop assistant.

"Yes, please," replied Loren.

"Are you new to Vladivostok? It's really a beauty. The first time I arrived here, I fell in love with the place. Ever since I have lived here," said Stacy.

"Not really, I was here before many years ago, I liked the place, it hasn't changed much though."

The shop assistant left, and Loren looked at the boat that has just arrived. Stacy returned with a cup of coffee and placed it in front of Loren

"Thank you."

"So, what brings you here if I may ask?"

Loren took a while to reply as she was busy with her coffee. She looked at Stacy as she stood in front of her.

"I am looking for my partner. I have the feeling he or she might be here in Vladivostok," replied Loren.

"You said he or she, does that mean you never met this partner of yours?"

"I never met him or her, but I have a gut feeling that she or he is here in Vladivostok. I have searched everywhere but I can't seem to find my partner. My husband left me months ago, he went to look for his partner I guess he found her or him," said Loren.

"You lost me. So, you are not looking for your husband. You are looking for your partner is that correct?"

"Yes, I am looking for my partner. Somehow this person is the key to everything. If I don't find this person, then I might die soon. When the time comes, you will understand."

"So, you are saying that your husband is not that person to save you?" asked Loren.

"It's strange, isn't it? All these years I thought my husband was my partner, but it turns out that he is not. He said I am not his partner. We lived together for more than fifty years. Months ago, he woke up in the middle of the night. He said it's time he has to go."

"Did he say where?" asked Stacy.

"He didn't say where the truth is that he didn't even know where this partner of his was. All these months, it never crosses my mind until a few days ago."

Weeks later Loren is outside a house in Vladivostok. She stopped outside and a strange feeling crippled her. She entered the yard and walked to the door. The barking of a dog startled her. She stopped for a while before proceeding to the door. She knocked on the door and waited. A woman opened the door as soon as she had seen Loren, she invited her in.

"So, you came for me?" asked Harriet. An old woman of Russian origin.

"Are you my partner? Are you the key?"

The two women sat on the couch and talked about life.

"So where is your husband?" asked Loren.

"Billy, left months ago, he went looking for his partner. I was very upset. After all these years, one day he just woke up and said that he was going. I could only watch as my world fell apart. Where is yours?" asked Harriet.

"The same story, he said that if he stayed with me, he would die."

Nikolai is a young man who has just joined the Ocean news channel as a reporter. He entered the office of his manager.

"Why can't you knock the door first like everyone else?" shouted Brad.

"Sorry boss. There is a lot happening in Vladivostok right now. I want your permission to go there straight away I think something big is happening there. I want us to be the first to report this. I want to be the one to cover this story." Said Nikolai with much enthusiasm and interest.

"What's happening there? You know the procedure complete the authorization form and hand it in?"

"I can't say for sure I will tell you once I am there. The authorization process takes long I should be there like yesterday."

"OK and let me know as soon as you arrive there."

Nikolai has been all over the place searching for interesting stories that will make headlines. The company was facing stiff competition from other news channels. Brad after weeks of convincing the directors employed the young enthusiastic yet inexperienced young Nikolai. The company over the years had relied on experienced reporters with a proven track record. This was a diversion from their norm. Brad knew they had to do something different to survive the economic climate. The company needed new blood to steer head their growth.

Nikolai arrived in Vladivostok early in the morning the following day. He checked in the hotel. After unpacking he went to have breakfast. In the breakfast room, there were other hotel residents too, among them Byron.

"The world has gone crazy," said Byron.

"What makes you say that?" asked Nikolai.

"Do you think what is happening here is normal? People dying like that. I have never heard of something like that before."

"What do you know about all these deaths? What are they saying is the main reason?" asked Nikolai.

"The world, just gone crazy if you ask me. Just yesterday two elderly people were found dead. Last week a couple were found dead together."

"What was the cause of death? Asked Nikolai.

"They can't say. Who knows? Even the doctors don't even know. Even if they knew they would not tell anyone," said Byron.

"Maybe it could be gas poisoning?" said Nikolai.

"The people are saying that those dying, they are committing suicide. The couple found last week were not even related. The woman traveled all the way from France. Witnesses said that she was heard asking for her partner."

"So, they were not husband and wife? Where was the man's wife?" asked Nikolai.

"I understand she left him a few days back. The elderly women were not related too. You have to listen to this morning's news."

Byron called the hotel's assistant and requested that they watch the news while having breakfast.

The anchor-man on the television was about to give the morning bulletin.

"Can you please turn up the volume?" requested Byron.

"Two elderly women have been found dead. Foul play was ruled out. It seems the couple have taken their own lives in a way that seemed to be prevalent now in the city of Vladivostok and in recent months.

Just last week a man and a woman were also found dead."

Nikolai after breakfast went to the place where the women were found dead but there was no one to help him so he proceeded to the hospital. Nikolai entered the hospital foyer and approached the assistant at the front desk.

"Where is the coroner's office?" asked Nikolai.

The receptionist did not answer but pointed in the direction to the coroner's office. Nikolai walked following the signs to the coroner's office. After passing corridor after corridor he arrived at the coroner's office. He knocked and entered the office. A man in his late forties with a mustache and reading glasses is sitting in the chair. As Nikolai entered the office, the coroner removed his reading glasses.

"How can I help you, young man?"

"I am Nikolai I am with Ocean news; I am a reporter I am covering the report on the deaths here in Vladivostok. What can you tell me?"

"The world has gone crazy. This small town has

witnessed deaths after death. Everyone is saying they are committing suicide but the autopsy reports

are saying something different."

"So, what are you saying? Are you saying that these deaths are not suicide pacts?"

"To be classed as suicide pacts, these people must have agreed and done something themselves to end their lives. But in all the cases I have reviewed, they all seem to have died of natural causes. I still can't explain it but something strange is happening out there."

"What did you find as the cause of death?"

"Honestly in all cases, nothing. They seemed to have died of old age. There was not even a trace of poisonous chemicals or any foreign substances that can be attributed to their deaths. Everyone had suggested gas poisoning of some sort, but we sent people to all the places where they were found dead but nothing. No gas poisoning or anything."

"So, are you telling me these people came together to die? I understand they were not related in any way," asked Nikolai.

"You are right. In all cases, the other person traveled from far away just days before they were discovered dead. There are still a lot of things we don't know. I understand the couple from last week, the man's wife left a few days before the other woman arrived. What we don't know is whether they were communicating before this. How do they get in touch? What happened the night before they died? At first, we thought they took poison but no trace at

all."

"So, coroner what do you think happened?" asked Nikolai.

"I am a coroner I believe in science, but I think there are still a lot of things man has not explored fully. Why would someone travel miles to come and die here? The strange thing is that, for all those who died. I checked their blood groups, their DNA, all the biological aspects. I must say it's a bit disturbing. Somehow, they are all similar. Same blood group same chromosome and DNA make up."

"Are you saying they are genetically somehow?

similar?"

"That's correct."

Later that day Nikolai is at the platform facing the Golden Bridge in Vladivostok. He stood there admiring the bridge. A young man came and stood beside him. The two stood there for a while.

"That's one beautiful bridge there," said Nikolai.

"A few years back the city was divided by the river. It took hours to reach the other end. Now in minutes by bus or car you can reach the other side," said Pedro.

"Mankind always there to make life simple and easy to live. That's great don't you think so?"

"Yes, I agree but also this has become a death spot. Just a few months it opened, a boy and a man jumped to their deaths. Over the years, the number of people dying has risen. The strange thing is that people are dying in pairs. The so-called, suicide pacts."

"Really? Something strange is happening. The world is changing. An evil spirit is among the people. Were the man, and the boy related?"

"As far as I know, no?"

Nikolai left the Golden Bridge and headed back to his hotel room. He picked up the phone and dialed a number. The phone rang for some time before going to voicemail. Nikolai cuts the line without leaving a message. He rang another number.

"Hello, it's Nikolai. Check the fax machine for an

update on that story I told you about."

"Did you find out why these people are dying. Is it suicide?" asked Brad.

"As per the coroner, they were all natural old-age deaths."

"Dying in pairs? So, all those who died were they all old?"

"I have a lead on another case that involved a young boy and an older man. I will check with the hospital for more information. Update tomorrow check the fax machine."

After the conversation, Nikolai placed the telephone down. He lay on the hotel bed for a while. After a few minutes, the phone rings. He quickly picked up the phone.

"Hello, Nikolai speaking."

"Yes, it's the coroner you rung me how can I be of help?"

"Oh, yes. I need information regarding a man and a boy who jumped off the Golden bridge some years ago, were they related can you check their DNA information?"

"Mr. Nikolai, you are asking me for something that

happened years ago. Even if I can access the files, it takes time. This is not a big city. Plus, I can't say that kind of information over the phone. Why not come to my office say Friday noon?"

Soon after the line went dead.

"Hello? Hello?"

Miles away in the United States of America it's sunny and a lovely day. In one of the suburbs, a car entered the driveway. A man got out of the car and opened the back door. He took out a suit and a briefcase. He closed the car doors and entered the house. Zack is a city accountant. Some days he finishes work early. He is married to Gabrielle. They have a son called Fredrick. A brilliant kid full of promises. Zack entered the house.

"Hello sweetie I am home," shouted Zack.

"Yes, please can you go and pick up our son? I am in the shower I haven't been myself today. `` shouted Gabrielle from the bathroom.

"Okay sweetie I will set off straight away," said Zack leaving the house. He entered his car and drove away heading to the school.

He arrived outside the city and waited. Other cars piled in front outside the school. Zack looked at his watch and waited in the car. Minutes later the bell rang, and kids started coming out of the school. Zack looked at the school gate looking for his son. Other parents without cars entered the schoolyard. Minutes passed-by without any sign of Fredrick. The time Zack got out of the car; he saw his son talking to an old man. The man then started walking away as soon as he saw Zack calling Fredrick. Fredrick came running and entered the car.

"I was looking for a mum's car. Why didn't she come to pick me up? I thought you were still at work," said Fredrick.

Zack made sure his son was ready before driving off.

"So how was school? Have you made friends yet?"

"School is okay. We are learning new things every day. The teacher today brought a frog to class. Daddy, you should buy one for me. You should have seen what the frog was doing. I asked the teacher if I can take it home."

"So, what did he say?" asked Zack.

"He gave it instead to the other girl who answered all his questions correctly?"

"So, who was that old man you were talking to?" asked Zack.

"He said that he was looking for his partner?"

Zack looked at his son and quickly indicated to come out of the road. He stopped the car.

"What did he actually say?"

"He said that he was looking for his partner. He asked me if I was his partner. I think he was looking for his son because I saw him in the schoolyard even before school was over."

"Are you sure that is what he said?"

"Yes, daddy."

Zack quickly started the car and turned around heading back to school. He stopped the car and jumped out of the car.

"Stay here close all the doors I will be back."

Zack entered the schoolyard and looked everywhere for the old man. He came out of school. He looked to the left and then to the right but there was no one. The man had disappeared. Zack went back to the schoolyard and straight to the head teacher's office.

"There was a strange old man, and I have found out that he asked my son if he was his partner don't you think that's a bit odd?" said Zack.

"Come sit down Mr..?" said Duncan the head of the school, pointing at the seat in his office.

"When did this happen? Did you see the man? Are you sure he was not one of the parents looking for his kids? We have a lot of people coming to the school, but I assure you this one is one of the safest schools around."

"He was a very old man,"

"We have grandparents, nannies, babysitters I mean all kinds of people coming to collect their kids. In most cases, if the parent can't collect their kid, they normally send someone else. He could have been a grandparent. Old age plays a key role too. It could just be a slip of the tongue."

Zack stood up and said goodbye with the head-teacher and left after that explanation. He got into the car and drove home with his son.

"If you see that man again tell your teacher or go to the head of the school and tell him, okay?"

"Okay, daddy."

The car drove up the road heading to the nearby suburbs.

Duncan is in his office and it is nearly time to go home. He looked outside through the window and saw an old man standing at the school gate. He remembered talking to Zack. He looked outside and walked out of the office. He approached the man but as soon as the man saw him the man started walking away. Duncan ran after him and tried to introduce himself, but the man refused to talk he kept walking away. Duncan stopped and started walking back to the school. He picked up the phone and dialed the school security guards.

"It's me, from today can you assign someone to patrol the school grounds. Can that be on a daily basis, especially during school days? There has been an incident we have to make sure that no harm befalls the kids."

Zack is in the bedroom and he is talking to his wife.

"You should go and pick up our son on time from school." Said Zack.

"What happened? You know I always do sweetie. Is he okay?"

"I don't know, maybe I am just overreacting. I saw him talking to this old man. Maybe in his late seventies. I assumed he was the grandparent of one of the pupils, so I drove off. It was on the way that Fredrick told me that the old man was asking him if he was his partner?"

"Partner? Are you sure?" asked Gabrielle.

"So, I went back to look for that old man to ask him what that was about. But he was nowhere to be seen. But I spoke to the head of the school. He said it could have been the grandparent of one of the

pupil."

"Maybe but still I will be on time."

CHAPTER THREE

A dark car arrived outside a walled building with a huge fence and huge gates. There is a security guard outside the place. As the car approached, he spreads his hand gesturing the car to stop. He walked next to the drivers' door.

The tinted window of the car slowly opened and a woman wearing dark glasses is on the steering wheel.

"Name and ID," asked the security guard.

"Joyce."

The woman stretched her hand and gave the guard her ID.

"OK proceed."

The camera on top of the gate wall moved and aimed at the car. The woman took off her shades and looked into the camera. The security guard gave the thumbs-up sign and the automatic gates started opening. The car entered the compound. Soon the gates closed. She drove the car and parked the car at the top of the building. She entered the lifts, and the lifts went down.

She used the pass given to her by the security guard and entered the building. She walked to the reception. There was a machine at the reception. She entered the details of the person she wanted to see. A list of names came up. She chose the one she was after and scrolled down. She pressed a button, and a message appeared on the screen. She went to sit down. She looked around everywhere. A door opened, and a woman came out and spoke to her.

"He can see you now please follow me."

Joyce got up and followed the woman. They passed several doors before going down in the lifts. They arrived and a big door opened only after the woman had swiped her card. Inside the temperature was a bit cool.

"You need these." Said the woman giving Joyce an overall, a hat and gloves." She pointed to the sanitization corner. Joyce after wearing her given gear walked to the sterilizing area. She washed her hands and wore the gloves. A man walked toward her.

"Just imagine if you can stop people from aging let alone from dying. Since the beginning of time, no man has ever managed to prolong life and maintain youth. It's my dream and the day that happens mankind will celebrate," said Joseph.

"It's impossible that's why no one has ever managed

to do that," replied Joyce.

"That's what everyone said before the spaceship landed on the moon. This will be more than landing on the moon. Just imagine achieving that in our lifetime."

"Sure, that will be something. If and only if you can manage."

"So, what did you bring me?" asked Joseph.

"I got the genetic makeup of both the deceased. It is strikingly similar. They were not related and did not know each other until that day."

"I have analyzed our animal subjects there is still a big difference between each one of them. The genetic characteristics are similar, but the makeup of their chromosomes is different. There are thousands of variations so to find a perfect match is difficult if not impossible."

"In other words, your subjects will end up dead?"

"Correct," replied Joseph.

Gabrielle finished taking a bath, dressed up and entered her car. She phoned Zack.

"Sweetie I am going to pick up Fredrick after that I am going to my sister's house. I will be home a little late. If you want after work come straight to my sisters' then we can come home together."

"OK, darling have a nice one."

Gabrielle drove her car to the school. After three in the afternoon, was the busiest time on that stretch of the road. Everyone is heading to the school to pick up their kids. Gabrielle wore her sunglasses stopping here and there in the traffic queue. She switched the radio on. Minutes later a bird flew straight smashing the corner of her window screen. She stopped the car on the roadside. Soon after she was back on her way. She approached the school in her car and parked outside. She waited for her son. The bell rang and kids started running out of the school. She looked at the schoolyard and saw her son coming out of school, walking with his friends. Suddenly Fredrick stopped and looked ahead of him. Gabrielle looked in the direction her son was looking for. She saw an old man running toward the school as if running toward her son. Fredrick looked behind him and saw two security guards running from the school toward him. They heard the car screeching its tires. Fredrick looked ahead of him and instincts kicked in. He was about to run toward his mum's car when the old man ran in his direction crossing the road. A car appeared from nowhere. It knocked down the old man sending him up in the air before they heard a loud thumping sound. Gabrielle covered her mouth in shock. The security guards stopped for a while before they ran to the old man's rescue. Fredrick opened his mum's car and entered the passenger side. Gabrielle looked at the road ahead of her. The old man was surrounded by two security guards. The old man was trying to get up the time the driver of the car that hit him arrived at the scene.

"Stay here lock the doors," said Gabrielle getting out of the car. She walked toward the scene hesitantly.

"Stay down, the ambulance is on its way," said one of the security guards.

The old man tried to get up. He constantly looked at Fredrick. The security guards kept holding him down.

"Let me go. He is my partner. He is the key. I will die without him. Let me just talk to him," said the old man.

"What is going on? Why is he chasing after my son? (looking at the old man) Who are you? What do you want?" asked Gabrielle.

"Let me go right now. There is not enough time. I will die. Let me talk to him?"

"Who are you?" asked Gabrielle.

The man did not reply he kept looking toward

Fredrick.

The security guards this time hold the old man down tight fearing that he might have suffered some injuries. The old man stopped moving for a while and looked at Gabrielle.

"He is my partner. Without him I will die?" said the old man before he closed his eyes. The siren of the ambulance was heard from a distance.

"Is he sleeping?" asked Gabrielle.

Both security guards looked at each other and removed their hands from his body. One of them quickly checked if he was still breathing.

"He is dead!"

Said the security guard kneeling on the floor looking up at Gabrielle who was standing next to them.

"Dead? Really! It didn't seem that bad."

The other security guard checked him too.

"He is gone. I can't believe it. He is dead."

Gabrielle quickly turned around and looked at her car. She looked like she had seen a ghost. Her son was sat on the passenger seat the last time she checked. He was no longer there. She started running toward the car. She opened the car door.

A woman's screaming sound startled everyone. In shock, everyone looked at Gabrielle. She quickly ran to the passenger door and checked her son. The two security guards ran toward her car leaving the old man lying in the road dead. Frantically the security guards and Gabrielle tried to revive Fredrick. The ambulance arrived, but he was pronounced dead at the scene.

In Vladivostok, Nikolai could not wait for Friday to arrive. This was what he was waiting for. He had sleepless nights. Friday morning, he left the hotel heading back to the coroner's office. He was driving a rented car when his phone rang.

"Hello, boss I can't talk right now. I am going to the coroner's office. Can I talk to you after the appointment?"

Soon after the phone line went dead. Nikolai drove to the hospital with high hopes that at last, he was going to unravel the Pandora box. This time he went straight to the coroner's office. He knocked on the door and entered the office. There were files on the desk.

"Yes. Mr. Nikolai, I looked at all the cases that were dealt with by this hospital. There is only one case when the other deceased was a kid. In all the other cases, there were all old couples."

"Were they related? Did you check their genetic makeup?" asked Nikolai.

"Not related at all. They had just met per the reports in their files. The man had traveled all the way from Canada. What's not clear is whether they met somewhere else and traveled to the bridge or that they met at the bridge."

"Very strange, if it's all adults that can be understood but if the other is a kid that leaves a lot of questions to be answered."

"Genetics coroner?" asked Nikolai.

"Oh yes. They all had the same genetic makeup."

"So, are you saying that these people look for people who are genetically like them so that they both die at the same time?" asked Nikolai.

"I don't know how the man managed to convince the young boy to jump with him. In all other cases, it was death by natural old age causes. In this case, the man somehow convinced the boy to commit suicide."

"Why take a young life? This does not make sense. Why travel all the way from Canada to talk someone into dying with you? Why not just jump alone and die?" asked Nikolai.

"What are you implying? I never thought of it that way. So, you are saying that death is not what all these people had in mind?"

"Exactly coroner. If I want to commit suicide, why would I travel miles away first then kill myself?"

"I think you are right. The initial thinking is probably to save their lives by being together," said the coroner before continuing.

"But why go to the bridge in the first place if the thinking is about prolonging life?"

"Coroner, in this case, there are no clear answers. It seems this man wanted a companion."

"What I don't understand is how they identified people with the same genetic makeup as themselves. There is more to it than meets the eye," said Nikolai.

"What seems to confuse me is why choose to meet and die together."

"Somehow these people knew that they were going to die, especially the one who had traveled. So maybe fear drove them to travel to support each other and strengthen each other before the big day?"

"In all the cases, they were all strangers until a few hours before death. One report starts that one of the deceased just woke up in the middle of the night and left his wife searching for his partner."

Miles away Valentine is in the house with her friend Jacqueline and her best friend's relatives. Penelope is there too, and they were talking and had been quiet for a while.

"It's very sad and scary that both die at the same time but miles apart in totally unrelated circumstances. Was my other sister ill?" asked Valentine.

Penelope stopped sobbing and seconds elapsed before she replied.

"It's hard. I can't even understand it myself. My beautiful daughter was involved in a car accident. My other daughter just fell after hearing the news of her sister's death and died too. We must wait for the autopsy reports. I have never heard anything like that before. The only story I know like this is when one of the twins died and the other one then commits suicide. My daughter loved life there is no way she could have killed herself. She valued life."

Clara and Lorenzo after watching the news about the woman claiming to be the oldest person in the whole world are in the bedroom. Lorenzo is sitting on the bed reading the newspaper. Clara is sitting in front of her dressing table cleansing makeup from her face.

"Just imagine living up to one hundred plus years," said Clara.

"I think it will be boring. I remember years ago, this man after his wife died wanted to die too. When asked? He replied that living alone was boring. So, this is human nature we are born to live on earth for certain years after that I think all people will see no sense of existing. When you are old you won't be in good shape as when you are young."

"Darling, Lorenzo, what did that woman say was the secret to her longevity?"

"In this paper, it's written that she was claiming that it's because she couldn't find her partner."

"What partner let me read that?"

Clara took the paper from her partner Lorenzo. After a while, she resumed talking to Lorenzo.

"That's strange. She is still alive just because she can't find her partner. Do you need a partner to die? Some people will do anything to be in the papers and on national television. It's just so unbelievable."

"She sounded genuine though," replied Lorenzo.

"Darling, since when does one need a partner for one to die. Probably she suffered amnesia."

"One of the guys at work, just last week he was

telling me that his grandfather walked out on his grandmother in search of his partner. When the grandfather was quizzed by his wife, it is understood that he confessed that he was afraid that he was going to die. So, he left looking for his partner. When he told me that I thought that he was kidding."

"So, Lorenzo my love, did his wife, the grandmother confessed that he was going to look for his partner to stop him from dying or what?"

"As far as I know, he told me that the partner was the key to stop death."

"So, is his grandfather still alive?" asked Clara.

"No one knows, it has been months now. No one knows where he is. He never called. Just a few weeks back, his grandmother formally signed documents declaring him as dead."

Nikolai, days later he visited the port in Vladivostok. He spends the whole day enjoying the sun and the beautiful scenery before he headed back to the big city. The sea eagles flew over the port, boats came and left. Other people appeared busy minding their own business. Why this city? Wonders Nikolai.

He stood up from the port bench and started walking away. He saw a nearby coffee shop. He walked toward it as it was getting cooler. The sun was setting, and the cooler winds were gathering momentum. He entered the coffee shop and sat next to the window looking toward the port. For some time, he got lost looking at the activities happening at the port. What was so special about this city? He wondered. The suicide packs why were they attracted to this city?

"Coffee?"

Asked a tall lady with a big smile on her face. Her chest was halfway exposed. Nikolai ogled her chest before seeing her blush.

"Yes. Coffee please."

Quickly Nikolai looked outside through the window feeling embarrassed by his reactions. The lady who happened to be Stacy left to get coffee for Nikolai. She returned afterward.

"A lot seems to be happening in this small town. I can't blame the people; this is such a cool place to come and wind down. It's so peaceful and quiet. It is totally opposite to my city."

"Don't tell me that you are looking for a partner?" Said Stacy.

"Ah. Sorry for staring at your, eh, you know. I have been away from home for a few days now. It was just a reflex." apologized Nikolai.

"No. That's okay. I meant a real partner. This place for some reason is becoming a love hot spot. Many people come here looking for love or relationships. It's a small city. All young men have run away to the big cities looking for jobs. The old men are at sea fishing for months. The local women are left with nothing to do and plenty of time."

"I am not looking for a partner or love. I am working here. What makes you think that I was looking for a partner, apart from staring at your assets?" asked Nikolai.

"Some time ago this old lady came in and sat over there. She looked troubled. We talked for a while. She told me that she was looking for her partner. After a while talking, I found out that her husband had left her for another woman. So, in turn, she left looking for a partner too," said Stacy.

"How old would you say she was?" asked Nikolai.

"I don't know, late seventies."

Nikolai takes out his laptop and starts researching something.

"Ah!" he shouted.

"What is it?" asked Stacy. Nikolai did not reply instead he took out his phone and phoned his boss.

"Boss. I have got another lead. I must fly to the United States of America. Check the fax machine I will send an update soon."

Nikolai arrived in the United States of America, following an article on the Internet. He traced Gabrielle and Zack. When he mentioned that he was a reporter they both refused to talk to him. They were too upset to talk about the death of their son. Nikolai drove his hired car to the school where the incident took place. He parked his car outside the school and walked around the schoolyard trying to understand what really happened that day.

A security guard walked out of the school premises.

"Hello, can I help you in any way?" asked Vivian.

"Hi. I am Nikolai. I am a reporter. I am investigating how an old man and a kid died here. Do you know anything about it?"

"I wasn't on the shift that day and the person who witnessed all this is off duty this week."

"I will be grateful if you can tell me where he lives. I don't have much time soon I will be heading back to Russia."

"OK wait here for a while I will be back."

Nikolai paced up and down waiting for Vivian to

return.

Vivian returned and spoke to Nikolai.

"He said that he is off duty, but if you want to meet, then it will cost you."

"I understand no problem. Do you have an address?"

It's a beautiful sunny day in one of the suburbs. A stranded small dog is running down the road. The dog is dehydrating, and it looks exhausted. The dog runs on the road through the park until it is startled by two big dogs fenced-in at one big mansion. The small dog stopped and started barking at the two big dogs. One of the big dogs looked agitated and barks back at the small dog showing its teeth. The small dog ran alongside the fence heading to the big gates of the property. One of the big dogs ran alongside and parallel but inside the fence. The small dog approached the gate and noticed that the gate was open. Suddenly, the small dog ran away from the big house. The big dog came out of the property and chased the small dog. An old man from the big house is standing outside the window watching his dog chase the small dog. He opened the window and whistled. The small dog ran underneath the nearby parked car. The big dog stopped and barked for a while before returning to the big house. The old man watched for a while from the window before disappearing.

A woman entered the living room and talked to the old man. She is young in her late twenties, stylish, brunette and smartly dressed. She smiled first at the old man.

"Can you call the engineer and ask him to fix the gate? One of my dogs was outside chasing after someone else's dog. That gate should be closed at all times. Tell him to come straight away."

"Last time I checked he was on vacation. I will try again straight away." She smiled and left the room. The old man sat down in his comfy sofa.

The brunette woman came back and spoke to the old man.

"He will be here to fix the gate the first thing tomorrow morning. Anything else you need before I go to the city?"

"That's all for now," replied the old man.

The old man picked up the phone and dialed a number. The phone rang for a while before someone on the other end answered it.

"Meet me tonight at the same place."

Enrika is a brilliant, smart, gorgeous and educated young lady who worked for the big clothes shop in the city. After six months with the company, she has been promoted as the trainee area graduate manager. She is very excited as that was what she has been aiming for. Life seemed perfect for her. She was having all the things she had wished for. She was having the best time of her life until one night. She was about to finish work in the city when an old man entered the shop. He walked straight to her. Ready to offer the perfect customer sales assistance service she smiled and waited for the old man to arrive.

"Good evening Sir. How can I help you?"

"Are you my partner? I am looking for my partner. I think it's nearly time," said the man touching Enrika by the shoulders.

"Excuse me? You are mistaking me with someone else," said Enrika.

"No. You are my partner you have to come with me, or I can go with you?" said the old man pulling Enrika. Enrika looked at the camera resisting the pulling. Soon afterward a door was opened, and a security guard came out to Enrika's rescue.

"What seems to be the problem? Are you okay?" asked Marc

"This gentleman was just living," replied Enrika.

The old man was escorted out of the shop. He

struggled for a while. Then he started shouting something at Enrika. The security guard dragged him out of the shop. The old man stood outside the shop helpless. Later he entered the back of the limousine and he was driven off. Marc walked back into the shop. The other sales assistants just looked on. Marc entered Enrika's office.

"Are you sure you are okay? What was that about? Do you know him?"

"I am okay it's the first time I have seen him. I don't know what he wanted from me."

Enrika laughed with embarrassment for a while before continuing.

"He said that he is looking for a partner and I am his partner. That old man, me? He must be crazy?"

"He seems well off; he got in a limo and was driven away?"

"These rich people think that they can just grab anyone they want and take for themselves. Hell no. Not me."

"I think he didn't mean any harm, otherwise he could not have done it in front of the camera and everyone."

"Money gives others a false sense of power that they end up thinking that they can do anything."

Enrika is driving home after work. The earlier incident left her shocked, and a bit confused too. She kept wondering what the old man was after. Surely, she didn't need a partner, she was happy with Titus. The two were in love. Everything was going per her plan. She kept looking back and checking her mirrors if someone was following her. She parked her car and sits in the car for a while pondering the days' events. The bedroom light was on, so Titus was home already. She jumped out of the car and entered her house with Titus.

"You won't believe what happened today at work?"

"Tell me, what happened did you get another promotion. I won't be surprised you been on a roll lately. I must confess things are going well for you."

"You mean going well for us? Not a promotion this time though but daylight kidnap."

"You can't be serious."

"If it wasn't for the security guard, I could have been kidnapped."

"Get real. Who can do that in front of everyone?"

"This old man came into the shop today and said I am his partner so I should go away with him."

"Was he rich?" asked Titus sitting down feeling a bit jealous.

Surely it was only a matter of time before someone else whisked her away from him. She was the luckiest girl he had ever met. She was gorgeous and had a hot body. Sometimes he wondered what she saw in him. Don't get me wrong, he was handsome, no doubt about that but he had an average life. He worked in the city earning a civil servant salary. Struggling to save money for a vacation. Yet she had everything, and men threw everything at her. This could only make sense if the old man was very rich.

"So, did you report the incident to the police? He might have had bad intentions?"

"The security guard suggested the same thing, but I think there is nothing to worry about. He seemed desperate. He was kind of begging and pleading with me that I go with him."

A car arrived outside a house. Nikolai is wearing sunglasses, it's a bit hot. He looked around and waited in the car. A ball rolled toward his parked car and soon after a young boy chased after it. He picked up the ball and looked at Nikolai as he passed-by. Soon after a man, heavily built came out of one of the houses and walked toward the car. He opened the car door and sat next to Nikolai.

"Do you have the money?"

Nikolai passed a brown envelope and waited in anticipation.

"What really happened that day?"

"This old man for some strange reason was chasing after this kid. Out of nowhere, a car rammed him down. He was kind of hallucinating claiming that if he is not together with the boy, he will die. Minutes later he died. He just closed his eyes, and that was it. Gone. It happened in front of me and Mario. Seconds later the boys mum lets out a terrifying scream. She ran to the car. Somehow the boy died at the same time as the old man."

"Did he say anything odd apart from what you have told me?"

"Minutes before he died, he said that the boy was his partner."

The anchor-woman on the television is talking about the worldwide deaths of people in pairs and sometimes in groups. An old woman is sitting in the hotel lobby. A man walked in and smiled at her.

"Hey, you are still here? Does that mean you haven't found your partner yet?"

He giggled and laughed.

"Very funny, as if it's my time?" replied the woman.

"Everyone else is busy looking for their partner and you are just sat there," added the man giggling sarcastically.

The woman looked annoyed.

"It's a shame. Why are people dying like that? The world has gone crazy. Is it the end of the world?" asked the woman.

"We are too many if you ask me and not enough resources. With the way things are going, we will struggle for resources in the future. Nature has a new way to correct that. Why not go in twos or even in threes? Ha? What a genius plan," Herbert laughed uncontrollably.

"Have you been drinking? Why you talk about death as if it's a nice thing?"

asked Maggie the old woman.

"We all go sometime. Loosen up, will you? Enjoy while you can. Maybe, you are my partner. Are you?" asked Herbert unable to control his giggling.

"Fuck off! I am not your partner. My time is not ready yet. Why don't you do like all the other men and go and find a partner somewhere else?"

"Oh, I almost forgot. Lenny left you. Where is he now?"

asked Herbert.

"You are now upsetting me. Don't talk about my husband let him be.
Don't you have anything else to do than to nag an old woman?"

CHAPTER FOUR

A huge 4x4 car was being driven past a group of people holding banners and posters and raising flags. They all surrounded the car as it approached. They hit the car with their open hands running after it as it moved slowly past them. Two people are in the car. A man and a woman. The woman is driving the car, and she concentrated on the road ahead while the men's attention is drawn by the crowd protesting for some sort.

"What do all these people want?" asked Robin.

"They want the wishes of the deceased to be upheld," replied Emily.

"What deceased people are you talking about?"

"All the people who are dying in pacts, they are saying that they should be buried together as well. But the states' policy is to bury each person in his or her own grave. They want that to be changed."

"Has the task force been completed yet? We want to know why they are grouping in pacts and why they are considering dying in pairs. Is this some kind of religious or cult thing?"

"We will know the results of the task force by the

end of this week."

Brad is in the office in Moscow city. It has been a week since Nikolai left. He is going through the headline stories. Things are improving but not as much as he had expected. He heard a knock on his office door.

"Come in."

Cynthia a very beautiful blonde girl with curly hair walked in holding papers in her hand.

"Fax paper has just been received, Sir."

"I have another lead; I need someone to check the story and let me know by the end of this week. Nikolai is abroad he should have returned by now, but he is following another lead."

"I can go and find out if you want?"

"Really? That will be great to find out what actually happened to these kids."

Cynthia left Moscow for St Petersburg in Russia. She was nervous but excited at such an opportunity to spend time away from office life. St Petersburg is a very large city and a very pleasant city with plenty of sunshine during the summer. The city is a port full of tourists and local people alike. The atmosphere is that of happiness and enjoyment, but the recent events have left the locals speechless. A so-called suicide pact was discovered. Three people died together. They were young, unlike most of the deaths which involved the very old. Cynthia entered the hospital and follow the directional signs to the coroners' office. She knocked on the door and entered the office. She introduced herself and went straight to the point.

"What is the official cause of death?"

The coroner, a woman in her early fifties sits down in the chair and looked at the files first. After a while she replied.

"They took a drug overdose which is the main cause of death. They were intoxicated as well."

"So, in your opinion was this a suicide? All three deliberately and knowingly ended their lives."

"That's what all the evidence is pointing to. What has been happening was that people were gathering in pacts and dying of natural old age-related deaths? This is way different. I sent to the lab their blood samples to be analyzed. This is totally different. There is nothing that connects all of them. Different blood groups, different chromosomes makeup and although unknown to each other. It seems they connected somehow over the Internet. This is totally different from what was going on."

"In your view, how did the others ended up together if there was no communication or linking between the deceased?"

"Honestly there are a lot of things we don't know. I think they have a sixth sense. They just knew. They traveled miles in search of their death-partners. Their chromosome composition is similar in so many ways that it's just unbelievable."

"So, it's fair to say that in most cases it involved the old people?"

"You can say that, but we heard cases too where a kid or young person was involved. Their chromosome makes up still identical. We just don't understand why they ended up dying together."

"This morning an old woman was arrested after running after the car that was carrying the Senator. Sources close to the Senator suggested that the bodyguards took no chances. They suspected that she might have been a suicidal so-called partner as she chased the car carrying the Senator despite being told not to do so. As I understand it, this is the second time the same woman has approached the Senator claiming that he was her partner. The Senator is taking this matter seriously and sources close to him said that he was disturbed by all this and was left emotionally affected by this latest development," said the anchorwoman on the television.

The Senator was in his office when the phone rang. He quickly switched to a secure line and answered the call.

"Yes, speaking."

"What shall we do with the subject?"

"Keep her safe but somewhere far away from me for the meantime until further notice."

The phone line was dead after that. The Senator got up and walked up and down in his office. He looked outside the window. He took out his cell phone and dialed a number.

"Arrange an appointment I am ready to meet but in secrecy. Say tonight at 7 pm come and pick me up from the same place. OK?"

"Copy that."

Sammy was a brilliant young scientist who was fascinated by life and human biological studies. Chromosomes and DNA were his favorite subjects at school. After school, he established his own laboratory to analyze and try to understand the human genetic makeup and its role in shaping human behavior, aging and life. Over the past years, he had been requesting funding from the Senator and treasury warning people that the future can be blink for humankind. Over the years his fears were being unfolded. The last time he had tried to persuade the Senator to fund his research the door was slammed in his face. He had been following the recent developments in the so-called death-partners. He had previously predicted that at some point people with the same genetic makeup to the greatest extent will one day come together to cheat death.

Nancy a young research scientist entered the laboratory. She goes to Sammy who was busy playing with his computer trying to rebuild and alter chromosome structures.

"It feels like yesterday I was warning people about the threat or the opportunities ahead of us in terms of chromosome development. Just today the Senator had a near miss. Somehow that worked fine for me?" said Sammy

"Why is that so? How can that be beneficial to you?"

"Guess who is coming to town?"

"Santa clause."

"No. You never take anything seriously, huh? I am talking about the Senator. Guess what, he is visiting our lab and if everything goes well, we might, at last, get that funding."

"I am proud of you at last our dream can be realized."

Later that night a black SUV with tinted glasses stopped outside Sammy's Life Science laboratory. Two men got out of the car wearing baseball caps and jumpers. The dressing was casual with track bottoms. The third man remained in the car. One of them made the phone call. Minutes later the door of the laboratory was opened, and the two men rushed inside. Nancy led the way until they arrived in the basement lab.

"Senator, I am glad you made it."

"Call me Roy. I don't have much time let's get down to business, shall we?"

"Can we go in my office?" said, Sammy pointing at the office in the lab.

"You wait here," said Senator Roy to his bodyguard.

Nancy followed Sammy and Roy. Roy stopped and looked at Sammy.

"I am not trying to be funny but three is a crowd."

"Don't worry that can be corrected. Nancy why don't you finish with the research while I talk to Roy?" said Sammy looking at Nancy who seemed unimpressed about that suggestion.

"We are partners don't treat me like I am your tea lady, remember that, shouldn't I be there too?" asked Nancy.

"Don't worry when we are making any deals, I will call you. Let me get to know Roy first."

The two men entered the office, and the door closed behind them.

"I don't understand. Why me? For the past two days, this woman is craving contact with me. She is asking my bodyguards if I am her partner. Is this as in death partners or what?" asked Roy looking worried and concerned.

That's what Sammy wanted to see and hear from the Senator. This is no joke a lot must be done now. This is the real-time bomb. In his heart, Sammy smiled. At last, he was about to witness the funds rolling in.

"I am afraid so."

"But I am not ready to die. I don't feel any pain. I am at the best of my health in my life. Why me? Are you telling me that in the whole world there is no one else who can be her death partner?"

"There is only one person in the whole universe

who has the same genetic makeup to the nearest thousandth as she."

"Still it makes no sense. Why travel all the way from the north pole to die here."

"Some suggested that they travel because of the fear of dying. They are afraid to die and travel the afterlife journey alone. Who best to be your partner than yourself? The idea derives from twins. One twin dies, and the other takes his own life. No one can explain why but it lies in sharing the same burden somehow."

"Listen, Sammy. There is no life after death. I die now that's it. I am finished. Are you telling me that that woman if she dies, I will die too?"

"I am afraid so. She has been in your vicinity somehow you are now genetically linked. Whatever happens to her happens to you."

"Okay, over the phone last time you said you can help. How can you help?" asked Roy

"I need modern-day machines to be able to carry out my plan. These machines don't come cheap you know. We are importing these from Japan. All this cost money Senator."

"Okay, how much?"

Sammy took a pen and wrote a figure on his hand and showed the Senator.

"And you can stop this? Right? Never to see that woman in my face again?"

"I will need your blood and will be in touch."

The Senator wrote a check. Sammy and the Senator and his bodyguard jumped into the black tinted car. The car drove for some minutes before the Senator jumped off. The car proceeded out of the city.

Sammy was smiling all the way. He had never thought that his dream can be realized this soon. This was the first time he was going to interview the woman, one of the so-called death-partners.

The car arrived outside this secured building. He entered the building. After a while of passing corridor after corridor, they came to a locked room. The guard swiped a card, and the door opened. An old woman was sitting on the bed. She had her chin resting on her knees as she sat on the bed. She looked afraid and disoriented.

"Do you want me to stay?" asked the guard.

"No, you are okay. You can go. I will be okay." said Sammy sitting down.

He gave the woman a bottle of water. She looked at

him and accepted the water. A moment went on before anyone said anything.

"Can I sit here?" asked Sammy pulling the chair next to the woman. She nodded her head in agreement. She drank the water and looked at the door and then at Sammy.

"If I am not with my partner, I will die. You understand?" said the woman.

Sammy looked surprised. All along he thought that she was looking for her partner to die.

"Excuse me?" said Sammy.

"I am weak and old if I am not with my partner I will die. I need my partner. I have to be with my partner."

Sammy looked at her. She sounded genuine.

"Do you mean your husband? That's the Senator. Do you know that? One of the most powerful men in the country. He can get you shot if you are seen near him again. Do you understand that?"

"My husband left me. He went to look for his partner. Who is the Senator?"

"That man you are calling your partner. He is the Senator."

"My partner, a Senator? So, this Senator refuses to save me? What kind of Senator is that?"

"Explain to me what you need from this partner?"

The woman drank the water first. She lets out a burp and apologized.

Joyce and Joseph are in the laboratory analyzing the genetic makeup of the deceased. They have been working for hours now.

"Joseph what I don't understand is why the pairing? Is it God's way of balancing the ecosystem?"

"Honestly I still can't figure it out. Initially, I thought it's a way of trying to cheat death, but it seems it's just a way of choosing the companion for the journey."

"What if this holds answers to avoid death itself? We are overlooking something. It's a shame we haven't been lucky enough to meet one."

"What if we start anticipating who might be in search of a death partner then we try either to witness the phenomenon or at least try to stop it?" asked Joyce.

"Maybe we should start collecting the databases of all prominent people and try to predict who is in danger and who is not. We might end up raising the all needed funding we require."

"Joseph, you only thinking about funding I am thinking about stopping death forever."

The night seemed like a peaceful night. There is a cool breeze and there is a half-moon that seemed to have brightened the night. A dog can be heard barking from a distance. A drunkard can be heard singing. A police siren can be heard from far away. A dog appeared from nowhere and ran after a cat. The two animals chased each other past Sammy's Life Science laboratory. A man appeared outside the back of the lab and started smoking. It's Sammy. He looked in the sky. What a beautiful night he wondered. He looked up and smiled. He puffed his cigarette as fast as he can before he went back into the lab.

"Somehow these people know the answers to all this. Somehow, they hold the answer to longevity. What will be the purpose of coming together with someone with the same genetic makeup as you? Is that the answer to death?" asked Sammy.

"What causes aging and death?" asked Nancy.

"Inactiveness of cells to divide and mutate after some time. They say the telomeres once they are too short to protect the chromosomes from eroding that's when things start going bad. I think the linking of the two has something to do with it. I think it's not just coming in contact. That could explain why they all ended up dead. It has to be more than that."

"You think it's the mixing of the chromosomes? Isn't that dangerous in itself?"

"Who is best to be your double? If you are twins and one is sick will the other twin not be the perfect replacement? Likewise, someone with the same chromosome make up is your perfect substitute."

"Sammy, what did that woman say?"

"She said that her partner, the Senator, is the only person who can save her. I have the Senator's genetic makeup, shall we?" asked Sammy.

Days later Dylan had just finished work. After leaving the academy he had protected the Senator. He was one of the Senator's bodyguards. He planned to go to the gym after work and he had also planned to spend his day off with his girlfriend. Protecting the Senator was a tough business. He was on alert all the time, sometimes he just craved for the time to wind down. The two days he had as vacations were barely enough, but he loved his job. Later that night he was in the hotel's basement in the gym. His pager beeped, and he stopped training and checked the message. He continued training. It was part of his job that he is always ready to be called at short notice. The bodyguards all communicated even on their off days.

Fiona arrived later, and they went out for food. Later they returned to the hotel. After a steamy night, they slept. Three in the morning Dylan's pager went off followed by his phone. He got his phone and answered the call. Without saying anything he got up and left the hotel. He jumped into his car and drove off.

Sammy and Nancy were working in the laboratory. The old woman was with them as per the Senator's request. It was after two in the morning that she woke up. She looked at Sammy and asked for her partner.

"Oh no! What's going on. We must live. Take her to put her in the car hurry up let's go," said Sammy taking whatever he can from the lab. Soon the trio rushed out of the lab into the car and Sammy drove as fast as he can.

"What's wrong she is not dead why are we running away?" asked Nancy.

"Anything goes wrong they will clean-up the place?"

"What do you mean clean-up the place?" asked Nancy.

"They will torch up the place. We are in danger."

"Stop the car right now. Let me out. I have nothing to hide. I was not there when you made deals. I will stay I can't ruin my career and my life because of that. All we did is try to help. They will understand that," shouted Nancy.

"We can be charged for kidnapping and false imprisonment."

"What? I thought you said that you had authorization. Was she not under police custody?" asked Nancy.

"No, that was just a cover-up. She was locked in some private buildings. Do you think the police would give us this woman to experiment on her?"

"Sammy. What have you done? You are ruining my life. What about the money?"

"Guess was embezzled too. But the good thing is that the money is in our business account right now. We can transfer it out."

"Sammy, have you heard yourself? Return the money. Let's come clean while we can. Let's hand in ourselves. They will understand." Pleaded Nancy.

"Nancy, we might be close to a breakthrough. You

want to throw away years of research and hard work. She might live. Let's just take her far away from the Senator. Everything will be fine."

It's two-thirty in the morning, a security guard is patrolling outside the Senator's house. The barking of the dogs can be heard from a distance. The bodyguard stopped under the tree. He lit his cigarette and puffed as he continued to walk the yard. He stopped and looked further at a distance away. Soon afterward, his pager beeps constantly the bedroom light of the Senator was switched on. The bodyguard ran toward the house. He entered the house and up the stairs to the bedroom. He entered the bedroom. There are other two bodyguards holding the Senator down. His wife is standing on the other side of the bed covering herself with a bedspread.

"Where is my partner? Without my partner, I will die?" Asked the Senator.

Josey the Senator's wife leaned on the bed and looked at the Senator.

"Roy I am here what's wrong?" she started crying.

"Winston, page Dylan, meet where the subject is. Clean-up the place and bring her here as soon as possible."

Winston left the house as fast as he can. He drove

toward the outskirts of the city after he paged Dylan.

It's early in the morning Liana is driving to work. It's very cold, and it's a bit foggy. There are traffic queues ahead of her. Cars are moving slowly. A boy selling newspapers is knocking on the windows of the cars asking drivers if they want to buy the papers. Liana wondered if that wasn't too early for newspaper boys. Normally they don't sell papers this early.

"Paper Madam. It's the additional edition. Buy one be the first to know," said the paperboy.

"The first to know what?" asked Liana

"Why can't you buy the paper first and then find out later?"

The sound of the horn of the car startled Liana. She looked in the road ahead at the same time picking up coins from the cigarette ashtray. The boy chased the car as it slowly edged forward. The boy threw the paper in the car and the lady gave him the money. She looked in her side mirror and saw the boy knocking on the window of the car. This must be big. What is it? She looked ahead before she opened the paper on the passenger seat.

"The Senator is dead?"

In one of the tall buildings in the city. A man well-dressed in his late forties with well-groomed sleek hair entered the building. He has a gown in his hand and a portfolio. He walked very fast entering the building overtaking people already in the building. They all say good morning Sir as he walked past them. Seconds later another man entered the building and ran to the other man.

"Sir, have you heard about Senator Roy?".

"Yes. I am aware of that. What a loss. Everyone thought that he was joking after that incident. Who is behind this? This is more than a coincidence. Someone is behind this. She might have been an assassin. I don't know how they did it, but I personally think that can't be tolerated? If it means killing all these tired people, then so be it."

"Will that not be inciting discrimination against the old?"

"Is it fair for the Senator to have died? Could you say his time was up? Or it's all attributed to the so-called death partner?"

"It's a huge loss, Sir. What is happening in the world? Are these new suicide acts?"

"You tell me. Just a few months ago, I heard an old man took with him a young kid. Is that fair? He had had his own life. He was tired and how unfair to take a kid's life? Where is justice there?"

The two men entered the lifts which took them to the floors on top. They left the lifts and entered the big conference room. A lot of people were standing in groups talking to each other. As the man entered the building everyone started taking their seats.

"Good morning everyone. I guess you all heard what happened to Senator Roy. Let's take a moment of silence in honor of the Senator."

No one coughed or sneezed after a while the man who happened to be the Chief of Security and Home Affairs Nigel resumed talking.

"Our country is under attack. All the people causing this are from far away. I want you to set up a task force to find out who is behind this. I want everyone about this to be brought to justice. Find out everything you know. I want reports on my desk by the end of the day. You are dismissed."

As soon as he had finished talking a big buzzing sound was heard as people started talking about this.

Enrika, left work one day, as usual, it was days after the incident in the store. She was not worrying anymore about that old man. It was later, on her way home that she noticed a car following her. At first, she just assumed that she was not being followed. After a while of changing lanes, she realized that she was being followed. She accelerated and the car behind her accelerated as well. Fearing for the worse she drove as fast as she can zigzag cars and overtaking. The chase went on for some time before she exited the road into a side road. She parked her car and ducked inside. The other car passed by and after a while, she continued with her journey. She arrived home and told her boyfriend. The next day she took a day off work. She spends the day enjoying life. Soon it was dark again. She promised that if it happened again, she was going to report it to the police. A big shining limousine parked outside one of the departmental stores in the city. The window was opened, and a man looked inside the shop. One of the men got out and entered the shop. He looked inside and minutes later he came out. He went back into the car. They waited outside.

"So, what do you want with this girl?"

"Somehow if I am with her, I won't die. If I am correct, we both shall live for a long time."

"Obviously, her yes, I agree, she is young. Not sure if I can say the same about you."

"I am telling you that this will work. Wait and see. I don't understand. If she is like me, why can't she help me? I am meant to sympathize with her so that in turn she reciprocates."

"She might see you as being selfish. You had your life. Let her live hers," said Bruno the bodyguard.

"Whose side are you on? Wait until I stop paying your salary then maybe you might think otherwise."

"I am just trying to understand this. This could not be good for both of you? I read another similar case like this where both ended up dead."

"Stop putting fear into me. This is the future. Just imagine people never dying again or living for hundreds of years."

"For the past two-thousand years, no one has ever managed to do it. What makes you special?" asked Bruno.

"This makes us special. Instincts. Somehow, we are linked. I can feel her breathing. I can't understand why she can't feel the same way. It's meant for us to just meet and link up without this begging and or this kidnapping."

"Excuse me. What kidnapping. That's not part of my job description."

"Stop whining like a baby. See that is the main reason man died for the past two-thousand years. Think outside the current norm for answers. Generation after generation man still trying and repeating the same failures with the same results. Listen to me. Today if this woman doesn't cooperate with us, we must take her home with us. Everything is set up. The idea is to do what has never been done before. Are you with me?"

"Yes, boss."

Minutes later everyone is in the limousine waiting outside. More and more people can be seen arriving and walking in the city. Bruno looked in the side mirror and saw a car parking not far from them. The woman in the car is Enrika. As soon as she had seen the limousine, she panicked and remained in the car. She looked at the limousine and noticed that there were people in the limousine as she could see the reflections. She saw the back door of the limousine opening and that old man from the previous encounter came out. He started walking toward her car. She looked behind her and quickly reversed. She drove off not knowing exactly what to do. The old man jumped into the limo and the limo chased after Enrika's car. It was still foggy and misty that morning. Enrika drove as fast as she can. She searched for her cell phone in her handbag while driving. The car served from side to side at one point nearly bumping into the oncoming traffic.

"Titus, I am being chased by that old man he is in a limo, I am coming back home call the police."

She threw the cell phone on the passenger seat and

constantly kept checking on her side mirrors and the rear-view mirror for the limousine. At some point, the limousine appeared in her rear-view mirror. She panicked scared for her life she stepped on the gas. A car in front and on the other side of the road tried to overtake blocking her way before moving back to its position on the other side. Enrika reacted as soon as she saw the other car in front of her.

She swerved sending the car rolling off the road landing on its roof. Bruno looked from outside the limousine and saw the car upside down with the tires still rolling. The limousine left the road and stopped a few feet away from Enrika's car.

"Hurry to get her."

Bruno and Jayden got out of the limo straight to Enrika's car.

"The door is jammed. I can't open it."

"Drag her out the window is open. Hurry before someone sees us," said Jayden.

Bruno kneeled and dragged out the unconscious Enrika who had bruising on her head and hand. The two men carried Enrika to the limo. Soon after, the limo sped off.

Two police cars arrived at a house in the city one after the other. A man opened the door holding his cell phone next to his ear.

"She is not answering her phone, but she said that she will be here after a while. Maybe we should go and find her she should be heading this way along City road."

Titus jumped into the police car and the two cars left heading toward the city. The two cars proceeded to the city center and minutes later Titus shouted to the officers to stop, pointing on the other side of the road. People surrounded Enrika's car.

"What happened? The woman was taken to the hospital?" Titus asked one of the onlookers, but no one knew what had happened.

"We have a possible kidnap. Along a city road can you send backup over?" said the police officer talking on the radio.

A big SUV drives along the road to the city. Inside are four people talking as they head to the city. One of the passengers is a man in his late forties with a beard covering his face and wearing reading glasses. He put his hand on his face and caressed his beard with his right hand before talking to the others. His name is Zunis.

"What the Vice President wants to know is that is there a way to conceal or alter chromosome makeup to come up with a unique combination that can't be matched," said Zunis.

"Yes, I think it's possible. I know someone who has been working on this for years," replied Martins

"What I don't understand is why and how these people are able to trace their so-called partners when nurture can have a significant impact on chromosome makeup. Take two twins, for example, they can never have the same chromosome makeup because the way they are raised and environmental influence affect chromosome characteristics and patterns."

After some time, the SUV arrived at a big building in the city. A man was waiting for them outside. They took their staff from the car and followed this man into the building. They entered the lifts, and no one said anything, they all kept silent. Their escort led the way until they reached an office in the building. The escort was called Timothy. He opened the door for them and asked them to wait in there. After a while, the door opened and the Vice President Aija entered the room. A highly ambitious educated woman. The way she walked said it all. She walked upright with authority. Her strides were systematized, and her smile was a genuine smile. She was adored by many. Many saw her as a pillar of strength and charisma. People looked up to her. For all, she was the cherished and loved the symbol of the American dream. Rich, powerful and in control. She emitted charm and beauty.

"Gentlemen, our country is experiencing a new threat at a scale unprecedented before. We don't know how to safeguard against these so-called partner killers. Somehow, we must find a way to stop or control this. Who knows? The next person could be someone very important. Look what happened to Senator Roy. No one took him seriously. There was nothing he could have done some might argue. Most people are saying it's the work of the devil himself some are saying that it's God's plan and man should not interfere with it. But I tell you, gentlemen, you are the brains of this country. Your task for the coming months is to find a way to predict and stop this pairing."

Suddenly, the men and the woman started talking to themselves and that went on for some time before the Vice President addressed them further.

"Timothy will show you where you will be working if you need anything just ask Timothy. Any questions gentlemen?" asked the Vice President taking off her reading glasses.

In the city center, a man is preaching to the crowd. He is smartly dressed, and he walked from one side to another. People came and stood and listened for a while before matching off. Behind him is a poster written that the end has come. God will pair you and take you to heaven through death like he has paired Adam and Eve in the beginning. A preacher is a man in his thirties, smartly dressed in a blue and white tie, a black suit, oiled hair pushed backward with a white handkerchief in his jacket pocket. He is holding a bible. His name is Isaiah.

"Just like in the beginning, when God created man and paired him with a woman. God shall pair you when your day comes. Look in the days of Noah. God paired animals and selected those to continue life after the great storm and the cleansing of the earth of all evil. Many have sinned and don't be afraid. Those who are paired are lucky. They have been chosen. The end has come to repent so that you shall be saved and enjoy everlasting life with the father the Almighty God."

At a cemetery, just outside the city people are gathered outside as they bury their loved ones. There are two coffins side by side ready to be taken down. A car was seen coming from the dusty road ahead. A cloud of dust rises as the car approached. The car stopped some distance away from the funeral. A cloud of dust rises to the sky. A man wearing a sleeveless leather jacket and leather pants got out of the car. He coughed as he wiped off the dust with his hand walking away from the car heading toward the funeral. He staggered from left to right. The priest stopped and everyone looked at the man who is approaching.

"I don't want my daughter to be buried next to that killer. If it wasn't for that woman, my daughter would be alive right now. I was robbed. That woman killed my daughter. It wasn't her time. You insult me by burying that devil next to my daughter. I don't even know her. They are not related so why on earth would you bury my daughter next to her? Don't listen to her mother. Listen to me."

"He's drunk again. Why make things worse Casper? Let me bury my daughter in peace. That's what God has chosen," said Tanya.

"Don't talk to me like that. Did God tell you that? That devil took my daughter and you feel sorry for the devil who took her?"

Casper fell on his knees and cried. Everyone looked at him, it was very painful for him. Tanya left the funeral and walked to Casper, the two hugged each other for a while. Casper and Tanya are hugging each other, and two coffins are over the open graves and a crowd of people dressed in black gathers around.

In the news, the anchor-woman is talking to an expert about the recent deaths of people worldwide.

"Believe it or not for some strange reason people are grouping or gathering together before they are found dead. This is different from the so-called suicide pacts. These people I can confirm had no idea that they were going to die. It seemed they gathered together to cheat death but, in the end, they faced death. I was lucky to interview one of the deceased. I can confess to the people that this woman in question traveled hundreds of miles looking for her partner. When I asked her why? She said that without the partner she was going to die. After extensive tests of the deceased, I can conclude that they are genetically similar, a copy of each other despite not related at all or never met before. How did they find each other? How did they tell they had the same chromosomes? All these are still questioning to be answered. All I can say is that there is more to it. Probably this is the work of something higher than humans."

"You heard it for yourself from one of the experts looking at these deaths. What would you do if someone comes to you and claimed to be your partner? Email me or tweet on the address displayed on your screens. Ursula reporting for Ocean news."

Sasha and Pelagia are at work and they have just watched the news. They are having lunch in the office. They have been busy and are behind schedule. Having lunch indoor in the office seemed like the best option they have.

"That's really scary. Is that the new way everyone will go nowadays?" asked Sasha.

"If you look at it, I think it makes sense. Everything in life that really matters is in pairs. Two hands, two legs, two eyes. Two people can have a baby most people and animals live in pairs their whole life so why not go in pairs? You will have a friend even in the afterlife," replied Pelagia.

"The scary thing is the way this is now happening.

When it first began, it was all old people, which I personally don't have a problem with, but recently I heard stories of kids and young people dying as well. It's scary. Just imagine planning your life and the next day someone comes and says hey let's go, it's time," said Sasha.

"How would you stop that person? You know even though he is asking for help that you might end up dead?" asked Pelagia.

In the city center, a man is walking very fast looking over his shoulders. He walked into a gun shop. He walked straight to the counter and waited for the sales assistant who seemed to be behind the shop in one of the offices. The man seemed paranoid. He waited for a few seconds more before he rang the bell giving it several blasts one after the other. A man shouted from the back office.

"I will be with you in a moment."

The man looked around the shop. He looked at the camera pointing at him from one corner. He threw his eyes to the shelf in front of him, a field with all kinds of guns. He looked at the guns and smiled. He gave the bell another blast. A man with folded long sleeves holding a towel peeped from the back office. He looked at the man before putting the towel down.

"Yes, Sir how can I be of any help?"

"I want a gun with bullets right now."

"Which one are you after? And it's subject to a satisfactory identity check that can take up to 28 days," said the sales assistant.

The man dipped into his pockets and brought out a lot of squashed together notes and coins and placed the money on the counter. The sales assistant looked at the money and opened the gun cabinet. He put the handguns on the counter one after the other.

"45," said the man.

Moments later the man came out of the shop with both hands in his jacket pockets looking around everywhere. He soon disappeared. Further down the road, a news van is parked outside a line of shops. A lady in her mid-twenties is looking in the mirror stretching her lips and putting lipstick. A man with a camera stood beside her. People are gathering around.

"Are you ready?" asked the man with the camera.

"Just a minute. How do I look?" asked the lady.

The man carrying the camera raised his hand and showed the woman three fingers. The woman stood attentively and put a microphone near her mouth.

"Everywhere people are scared about the recent events. What would you do when faced with such a scenario? For most, the answer is simple. Buy a gun. Gun shops have seen a sharp rise in sales over the last few weeks or so. The events of recent weeks have raised questions about personal safety issues and the need to defend ourselves. Is buying a gun the right thing? I think there are a lot of things politicians need to address in the light of recent events. Yolanda reporting for Ocean news."

Miles away a crowd is chasing an old man down the street. A strong man from one of the houses has been punching the man very hard. Other people joined in, but others looked in dismay and anger. There are mixed feelings. The other men are wrestling the strong man stopping him from attacking the old man.

"Hello. I need an ambulance as soon as possible. A man has been badly beaten up."

"Where did this happen? What is your address?" asked the operator.

"Waverley road."

"Keep on the line I will send the ambulance soon."

Another man arrived and restrained the strongman. He pulled him back from the scene. The strongman is very upset he has been shouting at the old man telling him not to come back to his house.

"What is going on man? That's not necessary."

"He is trying to kill my wife. She is not ready. I don't want to see him again."

An ambulance siren can be heard from far away initially faint, but the sound gradually increased as the ambulance approached the scene. It arrived and carried the wounded man away.

A man is sitting outside his house in the shade with a gun next to him. There is a doll not far from him. A kid's shoe is on the other side. There is a three-wheel kids bicycle near the gate. A cat walked from the other side and squeezed past the fence and into the yard. It reached the kid's shoe and sniffed it. It looked at the man and sat down. It meowed and looked around before it started walking again away from the shoe towards the man. It reached the shade where the man was seated and rubbed itself against the man's legs. The man touched the cat and stroked its back. The cat jumped onto the bench and sat next to the man. It saw the gun and started licking it.

"No, no, no, not this," said the man taking the gun

away from the bench next to the cat placing it on the other side. Sometime after, the sun started sinking down. Drops of tears hit the cat causing the cat to jump away from the bench in fear. The cat ran away out of the man's yard and disappeared. Soon after neighbors heard a gunshot causing neighbor's dogs to bark.

Sasha and Pelagia are about to go home when Amos entered the office. He removed his scarf and quickly got the remote of the television and sat down.

"Don't change that channel we are watching that?" said Sasha.

"Wait, I need to watch channel seven something happened this afternoon."

Amos switched channels to channel seven.

"It is reported that police have shot down a man immediately after he had shot another man down. It is understood that police were called to a standoff between these two-men outside the house. Despite warnings, it seemed the man at the house shot dead another man before police shot the man dead. Police can't be reached now for any comments regarding the incident." said the newsreader.

Amos sits back and took a huge breath. He looked relaxed a bit. He looked at the ladies and got up.

"I thought it was one of the so-called partner killers. I wanted to find out what will happen when you shoot that person dead. Would you both die at the same time or only that person dies? What do you think?"

"I think only that shot person dies. They must spend time together for them to die at the same time. It seems in all cases they have spent hours together usually overnight to be found dead the next day."

"What really happened in the Senator's case? There are conspiracy theories that his death partner asked for him just days before he died."

"Did the death partner die also?" asked Sasha.

"No one knows, at first they were stories that she was arrested and in police custody. After his death, those stories were denied by the police. People close

to him denied any information about the so-called death partner."

At the police station, the two officers at the scene earlier on where the two men died are in the office. Their boss is not happy about the way they have handled the situation.

"I am not happy; you should act like responsible police officers. In front of the news crew, why did you have to shoot him down? Everyone is saying that he had surrendered, he had put his gun down. Who shot him?" asked Sergeant Mark.

The two police officers looked at each other not knowing what to say.

"See you can't even give me a straight answer. Everyone once to know what happens. People from the Head Office are crying for your heads. Just last week the Vice President spoke against gun crime and violence. You two today in front of the news crew you paraded yourselves as sharpshooters. I will know who pulled the trigger when I get the ballistic reports. In the meantime, you are both suspended without pay. Leave your badges on my desk before you leave."

"But Sergeant like we said we didn't pull the trigger."

"I don't want to hear that. You are dismissed I will wait for the reports."

CHAPTER FIVE

Sammy and Nancy had escaped before they were attacked. They had gone away with the woman who was the so-called death partner of the Senator. They had discovered later that their place was set on fire. There are reports that the place accidentally caught fire killing a homeless man who had broken in or who was thought to be staying there. Nancy had decided to stick to Sammy.

"I siphoned the money in foreign banks abroad. It is hard to trace so don't worry too much. Everything is going to be okay." said Sammy holding Nancy's shoulder.

"Sammy, what shall we do with her?"

"I don't know. What do you think?"

"Maybe just leave her here and let's go. We have the money we can start another life somewhere else. This can get out of hand you know."

"You worry too much. I can't figure out why she has been like this. It was going well until the last days.

She is getting worse."

"Give her more of that syrup?" said Nancy.

"It runs out and the Senator is dead. But you must confess that somehow it might work."

"Listen to yourself. It just prolonged life by a few days, how can you say it worked. Can't you see she is in pain?"

"So, what do you suggest? We just abandon her here?"

"Why not Sammy? She is dying. She is in pain." said Nancy.

"I think we can find someone with the same genetic makeup to a certain degree. We have the money I know contacts. I think we should take her with us."

"You don't even listen to me."

Sammy and Nancy were talking together. In the other room, a woman was sleeping on the bed connected to tubes. She was in agony she opened her eyes and tried to get out of the bed.

"Where is my partner?" she cried aloud.

A woman walked to the window and opened the curtains. She looked at the beautiful flowers in the garden outside. She walked back to the couch and sat down. She took the orange juice and poured some in a glass and drinks. She looked at the wall and smiled. She saw the pictures of her and her new boyfriend. She touched her stomach and even smiled more. This is what she has always wanted, her head under the roof and life kicking in her stomach. Everything has turned well after all. All her friends it seemed had wished her bad luck. No one ever said anything encouraging about her but as far as she was concerned, she never cared anywhere. She switched on the television. She was looking at the television when she thought that she saw someone standing outside the window. She panicked a little, but when she looked again, there was no one. She stood up and walked toward the window. She flicked the curtain to the side and looked outside but there was no one. She walked toward the front door. She opened the door and as soon as she opened the door a man pushed her inside. She staggered back inside the house. The man entered the house and grabbed her tight.

"I can't die when you are there. You are my partner. Only you can save me. Don't push me away please, listen to me. We are linked. I don't know how but you are the one. Without you I am going to die," said the man frightened and holding tight onto Shelley.

"Billy! Billy! Help. There is an intruder in the house, Billy!" shouted Shelley.

Shelley struggled. The pair crashed against the

furniture in the sitting room. Shelley elbowed the intruder breaking his nose. He released the grip, and she was about to escape when he grabbed her legs sending her crushing on the floor. She kicked him like a dying animal pouncing on the intruders' head. She crawled and was about to escape when the intruder caught her leg. She looked around and saw a candlestick on top of the living room stand and reached for it. She failed to reach it the first time. She pushed forward only managing a little but enough for her to drop the candlestick down. The intruder was rubbing his head with one hand and with the other hand grabbed Shelley's leg. She grabbed the candlestick and stroke without hesitance. The man growled in pain and released her. She ran upstairs and fell on the bedroom floor.

Billy came back home to find the front door wide open. The place looked like there was a burglary. It seemed there was a struggle of some kind. He switched on the light and saw blood on the floor quickly he ran upstairs.

"Shelley! Shelley!"

He entered the bedroom and found her lying on the floor. She was bleeding from the head. She grabbed and checked her pulse. She was breathing. He quickly took her downstairs, into the car and drove off to the hospital. Halfway on the way she woke up.

"Billy, where were you? I nearly got killed by an intruder today. Oh, Billy never leave me again. Promise."

"I promise babe. Don't worry you are going to be alright."

Days after Shelley returned home from the hospital feeling much better. She was still traumatized though. She dreaded staying in the house alone. They sat in the living room talking.

"Cutie pie, how are you feeling? I took time off work. A few days together should do the magic. What do you think?"

"Sounds good, but honestly I want to go and stay with my sister for a few weeks. I am scared to stay here alone. In case that person returns again when you are not here."

"Don't worry about that, we called the police if he comes again, we just call the police. They also said that if he wanted to harm you, he could have done so. I just don't understand what he wants. I thought that he was one of the tenants living here before I bought the house. Whatever it is you are going to be okay. I promise. I am off work until next week after that if you want to visit your sister that would be great. Whatever makes you happy."

Just as they were talking, they heard the noises

made as if someone was trying to open the door.
Minutes later the top window panel of the sitting
room is smashed down. Shelley screamed getting up
from the couch standing near the living room door.
The curtains were flicked aside, and a man peeped
through the window with his eyes wide opened. The
moment Shelley's eyes met this man's she
screamed in terror and ran upstairs. The man
climbed the window and half his body was inside
the house. Billy confused at first what to do tried to
call the police for help but puts the phone down and
rushed toward the window. He started pushing the
man outside and punching the man very hard.

Shelley lets a loud scream upstairs. Billy ran
upstairs only to find Shelley bleeding from the nose
and slumped to the ground. Billy ran back
downstairs to find the man lying on the living room
floor. The intruder got up and ran after Billy who in
turn ran out of the living room. He held the living
room door. The man pulled the door hard. Billy put
one of his legs on the door frames and hold the
door.

"Shelley call the police! Call the police babe!"
shouted Billy.

Soon afterward the pressure from the door lessened.
Billy peeped inside the living room and saw the
man climbing out of the window. Instincts kicked in
and he ran toward the window and grabbed the man
by the belt of his trousers so that he can't escape.

The intruder struggled and, in the process, kicked him in the face. The man fell outside, Billy heard a huge thumping sound. He rushed outside, but the man was gone. Billy rushed upstairs.

"Don't hit him I don't feel good. Let him go," pleaded Shelley.

"Why are you bleeding?"

"Just don't hit him I feel like you were hitting me. Let him go."

"Did you call the police?" asked Billy.

"Yes, I have already called them."

Minutes later Billy and Shelley heard a siren outside and an urgent knock on the door. Billy got up and rushed toward the door.

"Yes, come in."

"Did you call the police? Where is Shelley?"

"Yes, we called the police. There was an intruder, but he ran away just before you got here. This is not the first time. Just a few days he was here. He attacked my wife. We were to the hospital, but she is okay."

"Why you didn't report this to the police the first

time."

"The intruder begged for help from my wife. She was traumatized but didn't expect the intruder to return."

"We will need to make a statement if that's okay."

One of the officers stayed with the couple and the other went to wait outside.

Minutes later the other officer opened the door and called the other officer out. The two officers returned inside the house. Can you both walk to the window and look outside? There is a man standing outside. Tell us if he is the man who is traumatizing you. The couple looked at each other and walk together toward the window. They slowly opened the curtain and looked outside.

"Yes, it's him," shouted Shelley hugging Billy.

"Something is wrong darling; Billy are you listening to me? What if I am connected to him? I don't understand how I was bleeding. Last time I hit him in the head but I blacked-out as well. I am scared."

"Did he say what he wanted?" asked the police officer.

Shelley sat down on the couch looking worried and

confused.

"Not really. The first time he was begging me. He told me that he will die if we are not together. He grabbed me very tight even now if I think about it. He seemed very afraid."

"OK, you two stay here. We will be back."

The police officers left the house and chased after the man.

Shelley and Billy rushed to the window to watch what was going on. The man on seeing the two men running toward him, he turned around and started running away.

"I need backup we are along Chesterfield road. A Caucasian male mid-forties casually dressed is on the run send backup as soon as possible."

The chase was underway. The man ran for his life he knew if caught there was no way he was going to see his partner. He was about to turn the corner when a police car came from nowhere hitting him sending him flying in the air. The police officer heard a huge thumping sound.

The man lay on the ground bleeding from his head, nose, and ears. The other officers arrived at the scene.

"No, oh no," said one officer kneeling next to the man. He tried to stop the bleeding.

"Where is my partner? I will die without her. Please take me to her. Don't let me die. Please."

The man holds onto the police officers' uniform and suddenly he looked at the sky as he lay on the floor still holding the officer's jacket. The two officers looked at each other before looking at the other officer in the car. The two officers got up and started running toward Billy's house. They entered the house and found Billy sitting on the living room floor with Shelley in his hands, tears running down his face. They looked at Shelley and she was bleeding from the nose head and ears. She looked lifeless. The officers exchanged a quick glance.

A motorbike came out of the highly secured building followed by two other motorbikes, a limousine, and an X5 black BMW. All the other cars stopped giving way as the arcade of cars passed-by.

The limousine has tinted windows and is highly polished that its body and the windows are shining like a mirror reflected by the sun. Soon the cars disappeared around the corner living a woman standing outside the gate. Inside the Limousine is the Vice President Aija. An intelligent woman. A ruthless politician with brilliant ideas. What she wants is what she gets. A tough politician matching the challenges of her time. When nature claimed mankind at an alarming rate, there was only one person to withstand the winds of destruction. When people needed courage hope and an answer, there was only one person with the stamina and determination to see them through. Meet Aija, the Vice President. A symbol of the American dream, rich, powerful and flamboyant. She is one strong woman who has been in politics for quite some time now. She puts on her reading glasses and draws files from her bag. She flicks through the pages. Quickly she took out her phone and dialed a number.

The phone rang for a few seconds before a man answered the call.

"Can you come to my office later this afternoon to discuss the project? I will be happy if you can bring everyone with you, say 5 pm."

The Vice President placed her phone down and continued looking at the files. The limousine and the escorting automobiles traveled out of the city to a private land after miles and miles of forests and bushes. The limousine bumped its way on the muddy road going to a huge building with smoke coming out of the huge chimney. The building looked old from outside. One of the men in the X5 BMW brought out some wellington muddy boots and gave them to the Vice President. She wore the wellies boots and came out of the limousine. She tiptoed through the muddy road until they reached the building. A big door opened, and everyone entered the building. A lift took them downstairs. They entered a room downstairs where they were asked to remove the wellies. They put on new shoes before they were taken further down. An automated modern-day door opened. This lab was very modern inside with state-of-the-art equipment. A woman came out to meet them.

"Welcome to our life sciences bio-research lab that is the center of our biotechnology research and development," said Faye.

"In layman's terms what do you do here and how relevant is it to combating the latest threats?" asked the Vice President.

"We are in research and development and manipulation of biological life to the betterment of mankind."

"You mean you make biological weapons in other words?" said the Vice President walking around the lab.

"Still you haven't answered my question. Can you help to deal with the current threat?" asked the Vice President.

"There is a lot we can do. Just tell us what you want to be done and we will get down to business."

"Can you create or alter the chromosome and genetic makeup so that no one else can claim to be your partner if you know what I mean."

"That's a new unexplored field. We can't guarantee what will happen, but we can try to predict the outcome. Altering chromosome and genetics is dangerous but we are not saying it can't be done."

"Let me put it this way," said the Vice President walking closer to the lab research technician Faye.

"If I want my chromosomes to be given a unique makeup would you do that and how much will that cost me?" asked the Vice President.

"Let's see. You are asking me to give you a new life? How much is your life worth?"

The Vice President looked at one of his aid and coughed. The aide a smart gentleman wearing a black suit walked toward Faye and looked her straight in the eye.

"I think it will be reasonable to suggest that you manufacture harmful biological weapons. Or let me put it this way. There are possibilities that your so-called biological weakening or taming methods might not actually work. It can also be argued that some of these biological entities might rejuvenate back to the harmful state. Further still, there is a high possibility that some of these biological entities might mutate back into harmful organisms and or they can be resistant to your weakening methods."

"We take every precaution to ensure that…." said Faye before she was interrupted.

"In layman's terms, there are chances that some of your so-called harmless friends might actually be harmful after all and pose a significant health risk to the public?"

"OK, what do you want?" asked Faye.

The Vice President cleared her throat, and the aide walked away from the two women leaving them to talk on their own.

"I want you to make me a unique set of chromosomes that can't be identified or easily replicated."

"Leave that with me. I will need your sample before you go but that will still cost you."

"Money is not an issue. No one else should know about this or you are dead."

The motorbikes the limousine and the BMW X5 left the farm heading back to the city.

Back in the lab, an old man entered the lab. He whistled as he entered the lab. He had a newspaper and a jacket in his hand. He was wearing a hat and reading glasses. He swiped his card, and the doors opened. He entered the lifts which took him downstairs. He wore special gear from head to toes and entered the building in the basement.

"Ah, you are back, why so soon?" asked Faye walking toward Viktovha. She hugged him and he kissed her on her cheek.

"How is my girl? Everything okay? You seem startled by something that is it? You are longing for a time to go out on a date? Is that so?"

"No papa."

"So, what is it?" asked Viktovha.

"We had visitors today. The honorable Vice President. She said that you two go back a long way."

"The Vice President wants help from me? That must be something. Is she dying or what?" asked Viktovha.

"She said she wants a favor."

"So, all these stories about these so-called double killers are real. The Vice President asking for help from me?"

Viktovha walked up and down the lab.

"So, you agreed?"

"I had no choice papa. She blackmailed me but she left this check she said the rest to get it after the deal is complete."

Viktovha on hearing this sat down. In his heart, he knew what will happen in the end. All these politicians after they get what they want they will try to eliminate any loose ends. They knew each other very well. Viktovha had lived this long because he had nothing to do with those in power. He never wanted anything to do with the politicians he knew very well that politics was a dirty game. His daughter had grown up to be a beautiful lady and a great scientist. Fear paralyzed him. He was old, he had no time to play hide and seek. One thing was for sure though he had to guarantee the safety of his daughter somehow.

A black hammer car entered the yard of the farm one early night. As soon as it entered the farmyard, the lights were switched off. Slowly the car made its way to the farm building. The car stopped and legs wearing wellies stepped out of the big car into the mud and walked toward the door to the farm buildings. The person rings the buzzer. Minutes later the door opened. A lady took the visitor down the lifts without saying anything. They came to the first changing room. They washed and sanitized their hands before changing clothing gear. They got in the lifts again and went further down. They reached the corridor to the lab. This time the lady took the visitor to a different room. She offered her new gowns and showed her the shower room and the other room. The room looked like a hospital room with state-of-the-art modern-day hospital machines.

"Viktovha. How has it been my dear old friend," said the Vice President?

"Still up to all kinds of tricks. Some things never change. I remembered the last days in Russia together especially that night."

"Viktovha my old friend that was a long time ago. I saw an opportunity, and I took it. You should be happy you ended up with a beautiful daughter. We could be childless by now. See we both won. Look, here I am just like the old days."

"I know you very well. In fact, I taught you all your tricks. I never went for someone else's kid you know that. My daughter is out of this. I want you to promise me that my daughter walks out of this."

There was a moment of silence. Vice President Aija sat next to Viktovha.

"Your daughter could have been our daughter together. Every time I see her, I just wished she was ours, Viktovha. I swear I will see to it that she is safe."

"You better be telling me the truth anything happens to her I swear…"

"Don't ruin the moment don't say anything. Tonight, it's just you and me. Let us make up for that night I left. All these years you have been waiting for me.

We both know it."

Later Faye carried the procedure injecting the Vice President with the genetically modified chromosome makeup. After the procedure, Viktovha and the Vice President spends some quality time together. They talked and laughed all night, for the first time, Faye heard her papa laughing as if his ribs were to break.

"On a serious note get the money and go. You know the drill there is always someone who will trace the money. Go back to Russia. Start a new life. But send me a postcard. OK?"

Viktovha kept silent for a while.

"So, this is it. I mean us," paused Viktovha before continuing.

"Let us go together. Leave all this. All this work I did it for you that maybe one day you will come back to me. We have the money. Come with me, just like in the old days."

Aija touched Viktovha's mouth and kissed him.

"What we had was special, but that was a long time ago. Let it go. Look after your daughter. I have too many enemies now and I will not forgive myself if something bad must happen to her just because of me surely you will not forgive me either. Take the money and go. Don't make it harder than it is."

The following morning Aija woke up earlier and disappeared.

Faye is in the lab working on her research when the phone rings.

"Papa get that I am busy. Will you?" shouted Faye from the lab.

"OK. I will get it," replied Viktovha getting up.

"Viktovha, (a woman coughed) Viktovha. Something went wrong. I am very sick. I don't think this is working. You are in danger. The aide let the cat out of the bag. Leave now. You hear me. They are on their way. Leave now go."

Soon the line went dead.

Viktovha quickly rushed into the lab and took what he needed and placed these in a bag.

"Faye it's time let's go right now. Now they are coming!"

The two, father and daughter rushed around taking what they needed. They took the bags into the car. Viktovha waited in the car as Faye rushed down to the centrifuge to take serum samples they had almost forgotten.

"Hurry up Faye," said Viktovha to himself waiting in the car.

Minutes later Faye ran to the car and jumped in. Viktovha drove the car out of the farmyard and as soon as they were a distance a car passed them going in the direction they came. Faye ducked as per her papa's advice.

Later that day two men walked into the Vice

President's yard walking like soldiers in a hurry. They knocked on the door and flashed badges. They headed straight to the study room where the Vice President was. Vice President Aija was laying down on the leather couch.

"We can't let them operate and run places like that.

This is the twenty-first century. What on earth do they think they are doing making viruses? People have fought hard, billions spent on research and development to a better life and these are reversing all that progress. What will all those who died trying to make this world a better place say? This can't be tolerated in any way. No human being can be given the slightest chance to reverse years of progress. I torched the place up," remarked Dwain.

"We have new threats their research might save millions one day," said the Vice President.

"You can't say that. Look at you Vice President. You have been in bed the whole day?" added Dwain.

"I know him. This is the price I pay for leaving him. He is blackmailing me. He wants me to go with him. Get ready we will fly to Russia tonight," said the Vice President Aija.

"Tonight? Do we have authorization?"

"I am still the Vice President. We have authorization as long as no one knows about this."

"But with all due respect, I think you need more rest."

"Talk to me when we are in Russia. You are dismissed."

Dwain looked at the Vice President Aija before he walked out and closed the door behind him.

Faye and her father are on their way to Russia. Faye was sleeping on her papa's shoulder in the plane. After a while, she woke up and looked outside. She looked at her papa. All this seemed to confuse her. Why would she want to kill them after all they helped her?

"Papa, one thing I don't understand is why she is trying to kill us?"

"There are a lot of things you don't know my daughter. The world is full of evil people. People who will not stop at anything."

"Still papa that can't explain anything. You seem to be happy together. I don't understand."

"Let's put it this way. I did not give her what she wanted. If I had given her, we both could be dead by now."

"But you slept together? I have never seen you so happy since mama left."

"Your life is more important than all this. Don't worry she will come to Russia."

"What if she doesn't?"

"Trust me she will come. Me and her go a long way," Viktovha smiled and rubbed his daughter's hair before kissing her on top of her head.

Viktovha and Faye arrived in Russia. Viktovha suggested that Faye stayed with his friend while he took care of business.

He booked the room they last slept in together with the Vice President then a young lady called Aija. He knew that if she were to come to Russia that's the hotel to find him. Viktovha ordered champagne and fruits. He was sure he had an upper hand. She was sure she had eliminated competition. On the run, he had no chance to find an answer soon. Her team was already working on a chromosome altering formula. She could see the President begging her when the so-called death partners came knocking on his door.

Viktovha checked in using his former code name. Only the Vice President was familiar with this name. Covered in veils and wearing long clothes the Vice President checked in using her code name too. She booked a room on top of Viktovha's room. Later that night she arrived at the reception and saw a red envelope under one of the chairs. Viktovha had checked in. She bought champagne and went to Viktovha's room. She knocked on his door.

"I am coming," shouted Viktovha running to open

the door.

"I don't feel so good. I doubt that you gave me the correct jab," said the Vice President Aija.

"Come on in. Don't talk that can be corrected. I wanted to make sure that my daughter was safe. You kept your word so I will keep my promise too."

Viktovha opened the small fridge and took out a flask. He unscrewed the flask and took out a glass container. He quickly got his bag from under the bed. He sterilized her arms and gave her a shot.

"This is the antidote."

He opened the flask and returned the small container and took out another which he handled with care. Making sure that it doesn't tilt. He sterilized her again before giving her another shot.

They slept together and the following day she was okay. The antidote had worked miracles. They said goodbyes, and she left after requesting a sample of his formula.

Back in the USA, the Vice President, excited meets with her research scientist.

"Look at this sample to see if the formula is genuine. If that means not sleeping tonight so be it. I want answers as soon as possible."

Three days after the meeting Viktovha was back together with his daughter. He looked worried though. Faye noticed that something was wrong.

"Papa, what is wrong? You haven't been yourself. Are you okay?" asked Faye.

"I can't believe she trusted me. She changed for sure twice I let her down. I am afraid that she will send someone to wipe us out. It's for three days now. Nothing happened after the third day. I must go there she needs me. I have to go and apologize, and this time give her the correct syrup."

The next day Viktovha landed alone back in the USA. Full of guilty he headed straight to the Vice President's place.

"Dwain I am very sick don't let anyone in I don't want to be like Senator Roy. I am going to take a nap."

"OK Mrs. Vice President," replied Dwain.

Viktovha had never been this happy and anxious for a long time. He smiled as he walked toward the place. He arrived at the gate. The security guards were watching him on the CCTV. They opened the door even before he arrived. He smiled when he found the gate open and rushed inside. He thought that she was waiting for him. But as soon as he had entered the property the gate closed behind him.

Dwain got out to meet Viktovha.

"Wait there. What do you want? I said hold there or I will shoot you. Do you have any ID? Who are you?"

"I am Viktovha, I am a friend of the Vice President. I don't have ID but that's not important. I want to talk to her right now. Please call her for me."

Viktovha looked worried and started walking a few steps ahead.

"I said to wait there. If you move, I will shoot you," Dwain quickly radioed the chief security officer inside.

"I have this guy claiming to be a friend of the Vice President. What shall I do?"

A moment of silence elapsed.

"Ask him if he is a partner of the Vice President? Ask him what will happen if we refuse him entry?"

"So, are you like a partner of the Vice President? If I refuse your entry what will happen to her or you?"

Viktovha had not expected this kind of questioning.

"I can confirm that I am a friend of the Vice President."

Viktovha looked worried and hesitant to answer the second question.

"OK, what about the second question," asked Dwain.

Viktovha looked confused. What kind of question was that he wondered? He cleared his throat.

"If you refuse me entry, she will die. I have to give her something it is urgent and very important."

Dwain talked on the radio with the chief security officer.

"Did you hear that? He said that she will die. I don't know what he got. He said that he brought her something. What should I do?"

Dwain looked at Viktovha who was advancing slowly with all his arms raised.

"Stop where you are don't move."

"Hello Dwain, this is the chief security officer. I checked with the Vice President she said that she has an antidote she received in Russia. Shot him."

Dwain looked puzzled and confused.

Viktovha remained standing there but hysterically Dwain started shouting and yelling.

"Sir stop don't move. I repeat Sir, stay where you are. Sir don't advance or I will shoot, I repeat. Remove your hands from your pocket. Sir stop now I will count to three. 1, 2,3."

Viktovha looked confused all this time he was standing in one place in fact slowly moving backward. He looked backward. He looked confused, was the security guide talking to him. He did not move forward. His hands were raised all this time before he looked back at Dwain, he felt his neck being pierced. He staggered backward before he felt a sharp pain in his chest. The Vice President ran outside with a gun in her hand. She kneeled over the dying Viktovha and quickly searched for his pocket. She put her arm in his jacket pocket and took out the syrup in a glass container. She looked at Viktovha who looked at her and smiled.

"I taught you… very ... well."

These were Viktovha's last words.

Later that night Dwain was talking to the news crew.

"I was guarding the Vice President when a man shook the gates violently. When he failed to open the gates, he jumped the fence and entered the yard. He claimed that he was the partner of the Vice President. When the chief security officer asked me to ask him what will happen if he was refused access to see the Vice President, he said that she will die. He was begging to see her. But after what happened to Senator Roy. I was given an order by the chief security officer to shoot. I shot him twice, `` said Dwain looking shaken.

"So, how is the Vice President? Is she dead also?" asked the news reporter.

Dwain pointed at the door to the building.

"Why don't you ask her yourself. Vice President! You can come out now?" shouted Dwain.

The Vice President walked out of the office staggering a little.

"You look like you were suffering from a fever, but I am glad you are still alive. How do you explain that? As far as I know, in all previous cases, no one has ever cheated death."

The Vice President looked into the camera for a while without saying anything. A tear fell from one eye. She looked around.

"Death came knocking on my door. I was nearly gone," she paused and sobbed more.

The reporter gave her time.

"So, what do you attribute this to?" asked the reporter.

"Thanks to millions I have invested into research and development working with these scientists, from all over the world," she paused and raised her hand pointing toward the building. All the scientists came out and stood next to her.

"I owe my life to scientist professor Zunis and his team. After months of trying they finally found an antidote. A way to give each one of you, a unique chromosome and DNA make up. Years ago, they said there is no one with the same DNA as you. Recently we have found out that in the whole world there is at least one person who is identical to you. But trust me when I tell you that that person is your worst version, your worst enemy. He or she is death itself. I will let professor Zunis explain how his work is going to save you from the so-called death partners. Before I go. I want to tell you that no one is safe even the President is not safe. Is it an act?

God or the work of the devil? I think it doesn't matter anymore. One thing that is for sure is that it can be defeated. Professor Zunis, ladies and gentlemen."

"For months, night after night, we worked very hard

sleepless nights trying to save humanity. At last, we have figured a way to alter chromosome makeup so that we can make each and everyone's chromosomes unique. In the future that will save millions from death. Any questions get in touch we will be happy to help. Thank you," said professor Zunis.

For the first time in the history of mankind, the Vice President had more power than any President and Prime minister.

Weeks after, Faye received a check for millions of dollars, she sobbed uncontrollably. They had talked about this. She rather preferred her papa than bloodied money. She knew her dad had died; this was the sign. Somehow, she got really upset about the Vice President. Maybe one day she has to get revenge.

CHAPTER SIX

Sammy and Nancy are walking down the street shivering bracing the cold. Sammy is in front and Nancy is following him. Sammy stopped and waited for Nancy to catch up. She is shivering. The two hugged each other and Sammy rubbed her back. The pair continued walking in the street. They reached a park and entered the gates to the park. There is a bench in the park. Sammy stopped. He looked around and lit his cigarette. He smoked his cigarette looking in the sky.

"We should keep ongoing, it's very cold," said Nancy rubbing her hands together to keep warm.

Sammy ignored her pleas instead introduced a new topic.

"Somehow I can see the changes I am not sure how significant these are."

He dropped the cigarette butt and smudged it in the mud on the ground. The pair started walking again heading toward the exit to the park on the other side. They come out of the other street. Sammy snooped around and the pair walked along a narrow path.

A dog came running from the house along the path

sending Nancy jumping. The dog barked jumping at them on the other side of the fence.

"Don't you worry. It's fenced we should be fine," said Sammy.

Nancy hugged Sammy, and the pair continued walking.

"Holy Christ, run. Nancy run," shouted Sammy.

Sammy saw the opening in the fence ahead and the pair ran as fast as they can. The dog chased them for a while before it stopped and kept barking. Sammy stopped near a park bench breathing heavily and squatted, a few minutes later he lay on the ground. Nancy threw herself on the park grass and the pair started laughing.

"I have never run as fast as I did tonight, I didn't know you can run this fast too," said Sammy.

"Man, that was very scary. I panicked. I didn't see the opening until the last minute."

"Are you still feeling cold?"

"No. I feel like taking my jumper off. It feels good after all these months of worrying just to relax and be ourselves."

"I thought you were a dog person."

"Eh, you can say that but not that kind of dog."

The pair lay in the park for a while looking up in the sky observing the stars and the moon.

"How long are we going to be like this? I miss home I miss my cat I crave Chinese and cuddling on the couch, watching a movie, you know?"

Sammy kept silent he just looked at Nancy and touched her forehead pushing her hair backward.

"My plan is to find out what makes these people travel from far away looking for someone nearly identical to them, genetic wise. I think we are missing something, or we are overlooking something."

"We will find out soon if there have been any improvements," said Nancy.

After a while, the pair got up and walked to a house with huge walls.

Weeks later, the pair after their usual rounds came back home to find that the place had been broken into. The front door was forced open. Sammy rushed upstairs to check on the woman they were looking after. The door to her room was broken as well. She was lying on the bed with her eyes wide open. The drip stand was on the floor. It seems there has been a struggle of some kind. Nancy ran upstairs and slides the door open. She stopped at the door before sitting down next to the dead woman. She looked at her blouse which was open halfway through. Nancy quickly opened her blouse after noticing something unusual. Her body had rejuvenated. Her face looked old, but her body's skin looked smooth.

"Sammy, I think you might want to see this?"

"What is it?" asked Sammy getting up from the chair in the room walking toward the bed.

"Hey so somehow this was working."

"I think someone strangled her. We are not safe here. We have to go," said Nancy.

"Wait, I need samples. We were close to discovering the whole thing. What might have happened."

Sammy ran downstairs and quickly brought his gear. He took blood samples, and the pair left the house.

A car is driving along the road. It is very big and wide. It looked like an executive's car. The front wheels came to a halt just before the line across the road. A man is in the car. Middle-aged and handsome. He is very masculine with a big chin with a dimple. He pulled down the mirror on top near the rear-view mirror. He looked at his face and his teeth. He flicked back the mirror, and the lights changed to green and he drove the car forward. He switched the radio on and drove for a while. He came to a traffic light and stopped the car. He looked to his right and saw a billboard with an advertisement.

The message reads;

'Imagine planning everything. Setting your goals in life. Working very hard and one day a visitor from hell comes and says your time is up? Are you well prepared for the surprise visit? Don't leave everything to chance. Get the jab now. Call the number below.'

The smile that was on Alex's face vanished away. He looked worried. The lights changed to green still Alex remained stationary at the traffic lights, in his own world. It was the sound of the horn made by the driver behind that woke him up. He continued with his journey. He arrived in the city offices and phoned his girlfriend. She was busy, so he left a message. Lucia one of the female co-workers knocked on the door and entered straight away. She walked in and sat at the desk.

"You seemed worried about something lately, what is it?"

"Nothing really just been busy as usual."

"You are not the Alex I know. You hide in your office nowadays. Come on! You can tell me what's really bothering you."

Alex stroked his tie and looked at Lucia. She was older than him, good-looking though with a lovely body. He remembered bumping into her with her European boyfriend.

"I was thinking about this jab-thing. Is there any truth in that? I am mainly worried about the side effects and the cost is very high?"

"Your life is more important than all these material things. You can wake up one day and boom you are gone."

"I think whoever is behind this is scaring people so that he can make a score?"

"Are you telling me that you haven't received the jab yet? Almost everyone has received this jab. Trust me no one will tell you in case something goes wrong. I had one."

"Really, how did you manage that?"

"I just called that number. They have arrangements with all banks and government bodies. The bank pays them cash you just sign the papers, and the bank deducts money straight from your wages monthly."

"It seems it is a must-have. The government is pushing hard to have this as a requirement for everything."

"What about the side effects? I understand they use weakened viruses to give your chromosomes a unique makeup. What if something goes wrong?"

"It's better than doing nothing. The Vice President herself had this jab. This will soon be compulsory and recently insurance companies are refusing to cover those without this jab. If I were you, I would get the jab than wait in the dark."

"I have to think about it."

A big limousine appeared from the corner of a street and drove forward before the driver indicated right. The limo stopped outside the hotel in the city. The usher who was waiting outside ran to open the door. The usher, wearing clean white gloves reached for the door handles and pulled open the limo's door. A pair of polished white shoes presses down the comfy red carpet. A man came out wearing a matching white suit and a black bore tie. He briefly looked at the usher before turning to the crowd on the other side. Camera flashes blinded his eyes for some time before he looked on the other side of the limo. A woman dressed to kill got out of the limo and looked at the man. They both smiled at each other and started walking hand in hand on the comfy red carpet going up the stairs. They reached the top level and looked back at the crowd. They both waved their hands. The woman kissed the man on the cheek and they both entered the hotel. They could still hear the crowd cheering outside.

"You look lovely tonight Vice President."

"Thank you, Mr. President. You don't look bad yourself."

The pair walked inside to the applause of the people surrounding the big dinner table.

"Thank you, thank you. You can all sit down."

The ushers drew out the President and the Vice President's chairs, and they sat down and everyone else followed suit. Later that evening the President walked outside through the open French doors. The usher followed him with a tray raised to the shoulder level. The usher lowered the tray, and the President took a glass of wine. The Vice President is standing outside looking over to the beautiful garden outside. She is holding a glass of wine too. There is a balcony and they are standing against the rails.

"It's lovely tonight. The atmosphere is great."

"Lovely indeed Mr. President."

"Seems you are doing very well."

"My offer still stands. Don't leave things to chance. We are still waiting for you, Mr. President."

"You are a lovely person Vice President, but I will pass."

"OK don't say I didn't warn you. Threats have changed. You don't know who to trust."

"If it's my time, then it's my time. I have had a wonderful life. I have no regrets, Mrs. Vice President."

"It will be a waste of life. Life as we know it is changing. Soon death will be defeated. Nowadays we are working on rejuvenating the whole person making you young again. Old age will be a thing of the past," said the Vice President.

The President did not say anything instead he sipped his wine and looked into the sky.

"That might be years away. By that time, we all will have gone."

"Have gone. Mr. President. Do you know the death partner of the Senator was still alive days after the Senator kicked the bucket?"

"Senator Roy?"

"Senator Roy himself."

"No. How is that possible. I am the President shouldn't I be the one to tell you that?"

"There are a lot of things you don't know."

"Then tell me Vice President."

"Somehow the Senator's blood was given to this death partner, and it rejuvenated her. The time she died her body skin had smoothed again." "What are you saying Vice President?"

"Instincts to survive brings these people together. It's in the early stages. There is more to it than meets the eye."

"Death and wrinkles will be a thing of the past. Imagine people living for hundreds of years. This is not like today when you live miserable lives in old age wrinkly and frail. This is giving you a second life and your youth back. Who will be behind all this? Me and after that the opportunities are endless."

"I never thought of it that way. I guess I need a rethink about the whole thing Mrs. Vice President."

"Don't leave it until it's too late. I would want you in my future world, Mr. President."

"The feeling is mutual. Shall we go inside and dance?"

The President is in his office. He heard a knock on the door.

"Come in."

"Mr. President I heard you sent for me," asked the chief adviser to the President.

"Yes, sit down please."

The President got up and walked to the display cabinet. He opened the door and reached for a small glass bottle with expensive wine and took two small glasses. He poured wine and carried the two glasses to the table.

"I don't understand. If I am the President, why am I not updated on things happening around me, especially ones that are so important?"

"Thank you, Mr. President (accepting the glass of wine). The Vice President has sole ownership of the research. She used her own funds to set up the project. There is no conflict of interest. Only members are entitled to the information and clearly, you denied any involvement."

"So how can I get information without being a member?"

"Without using your executive powers, I think it might be difficult. The Vice President has closed all the loopholes. Even with your executive powers still, you will need the approval of the Vice President and the courts which are all controlled by the Vice President."

"If I am the President, how come you tell me there is nothing I can do?"

"The Vice President is becoming a formidable force. Billions have subscribed to her jabs and her company. Every day she is controlling everything. They say money is power and stands to be true in this case. But Mr. President I am not saying it can't be done."

"Now you are talking. Go on I am listening."

Days later the President is standing in his office. He looked outside the window and sipped his wine. His long-sleeved shirt is folded. He stretched his arm and there is a small round plastic bandage on his arm. It looked blooded. He cursed and walked to his drawer and pulled the handle. He took out a small box and drew out a new plastic bandage.

It's night time in the city, the city is quiet but still,

there is traffic still moving. Two men are seated in the car. One is smoking blowing the smoke throughout the window. The other one looks nervous and kept looking at his watch. Across the street, a woman pushed the heavy glass door open and walked out of the building. She entered the nearby parked car and drove off. A beeping alarm goes off in the car. The two men started preparing things and wearing balaclavas. They carried a bag into the building. Quickly they ran upstairs into an office and switched on the computer. They linked the computer to one of the gadgets they had. They synchronized the gadget and the computer and accessed the computer through the gadget. They checked through the files and downloaded the files they were after onto the gadget. A car stopped outside and one of the men walked to the window and looked outside.

"We have company hurry up."

"I haven't finished yet still downloading."

The woman opened the door and entered the office and walked to her desk. She opened a drawer and took some files out. She heard a beeping sound. She has heard this sound before so many times she knew straight away what that was. She checked the computer, it seemed it had just switched off. She stopped and looked around. She walked out of the office and left. After a while, the two men jumped down from the ceiling air ducts.

"Can we go now? Did you get the files?"

"Come lets, go."

The two men left the building.

Miles away a small girl ran out of the house and picked up a package on the lawn. She ran back with the parcel into the house and placed it on the table. A dog came into the house from outside and started sniffing the packaging. A woman came downstairs and sat down in front of the package. She looked at the box in front of her and took the parcel putting it on her lap. She cuts the string and tore the packaging open. She took out a magazine and flipped through the pages. A small piece of paper dropped down. She threw the magazine on the table and looked at the small thin paper. She opened a bag nearby and wore reading glasses. A message is displayed on the inside of the lenses of the glasses and a circle is going clockwise as information is being uploaded. After a while, a message is displayed on the lenses asking her to wear headphones and connect the voice analyzer. She took out her headphones and wore them and connected a small device as well and linked this to the computer. A map of the world is displayed on the laptop screen. As the codes are converted by the reading glasses. A voice is played on the headphones and a message is sent to the device and a few seconds later the position is shown, and a triangle appeared on the map. It goes on for some time until six points are marked on the map.

A message appeared on the computer screen asking to save. The woman saved the coordinates. She opened another program and entered the coordinates. She sat back and watched as the information is uploaded. The young girl returned in the living room and jumped on the couch resting on her knees. She looked at the laptop and rested on her mother's shoulder.

"Mummy, can we play cast the spells now?"

"Okay first switch on the television and wear your magic dress."

The young girl jumped off the couch and kneeled in front of the television. She clapped her hands, and the television switched on.

"Channel Five," shouted the young girl, and the television switched to channel five. She ran upstairs. The woman heard a thumping noise, she smiled.

"Are you okay, be careful mind those steps."

The girl got up and continued up the stairs into her room. Minutes later she came back wearing a pink Cinderella dress that seemed to sweep the floor, a magic hat and in her hand a spell casting stick with a round top. She stood in front of her mum.

"Mummy I am ready."

"Okay, I am nearly ready we start now."

A picture of a woman appeared on the television at the triangulated place. As soon as it appeared the young girl shook the magic stick as if throwing a missile at the image. The image turned red and minutes later the image and the point disappeared from the screen. Another image appeared on the screen and the young girl threw a missile again soon the image disappeared from the screen. Somehow, she missed the last image. A message appeared on the screen asking for the coordinates to be recalibrated.

"Ah, you missed one. But that's great just wait for mummy to recalibrate the coordinates again."

A few minutes later the woman picked up the phone.

"Subjects down move in fast."

A car pulls up at the side of the road. A woman jumped out of the car and entered the house holding a gun looking everywhere. She opened the door and went upstairs. She entered room after room. She arrived at the bedroom door and slowly opened the door. There were a couple in bed. She aimed the gun at one of the couples and slowly advanced. She shot one of the couples in the neck. A needle protruded on the neck. She sends a beeping signal to the other one in the car outside. The other woman got out of the car with a small bag and rushed into the house. They took blood samples of the other one of the couples who has not been shot with a needle. Before they left, they remove the needle from the neck. They got back into the car and drove off.

A car arrived outside the building and two women got off and carried a small bag into the building.

"We got the samples."

The man flicked his fingers and a lab technician came and collected the small bag. He emptied the contents in a tube.

The man picked up a device and asked the woman to lick a protracted ribbon on a small machine. The machine beeps as soon as they have licked the ribbons. The man looked at the machine.

A message is displayed soon after.

"Money transfer completed."

The two women left the building, and the car drove off.

One of the women in the car took a small gadget

from her breast pocket and licked the film.

A message appeared on the screen;

Funds successfully received.

She puts back the small gadget in her pocket.

Somewhere in Russia Faye is sitting in a cafe using her laptop. A man walked in and sat in front of her. He slides an envelope. Inside is a magazine. She flipped through the pages and took a small piece of paper. She placed back the magazine on the table.

"Jabs are now a trillion-dollar industry. The most powerful woman in the whole world."

Faye looked at the magazine and looked at the front cover. The Vice President's picture is on the cover with the slogan; Don't leave anything to chance. Get the jab.

Faye slammed the magazine back on the table.

"She is a phony?"

"What do you mean? She has revolutionized humanity. She is saving lives. The jabs are working. She survived an assassination attempt. No one has ever done that before."

"She is a liar. She is tricking people."

"You think that all these people are paying her thousands of dollars for nothing. I myself had the jab. No single person has been that rich before. She has more power than the President himself. So, tell me how she is a phony?"

Romero leaned forward looking at Faye.

"I have gone through a list of the people targeted recently. The only reason that makes sense is that. The jabs are fake."

"How can the jabs be fake? They are targeting the death partners eliminating them one by one and nothing happens to the other partner. How can you explain that?"

"That's what I can't figure out?"

"Admit you are just jealous. You wish it was you who first made the discovery, huh?"

Laughs Romero sitting back in his chair.

"That was my papa's idea. But I can't figure it out how and why only one of the pairs is dying?"

"Listen get the jab today insurance can cover for it. Banks and governments offer free insurance."

Faye ignored him trying to figure out what was

going on.

"Okay let me work with what I know. I know the Vice President faked the assassination attempt which means her real death partner is still out there. I know and have helped develop her jab. Which means if I can find a way to reverse back the changes that leave her exposed to the real death partner. Romero! Can you come with me?"

The pair left the cafe. Minutes later they arrived at a walled house.

Later that night Faye stayed with Romero taking some blood samples and marrow from him.

"You are stealing my jab now. Do you know I still owe the money for that? I have to work a quarter of my life to complete paying for that."

"I am not stealing I am like an independent adjudicator making sure you are receiving value for money. I will take just a sample."

Weeks later Faye spent more time in the lab. She had spent countless nights in the lab. She couldn't figure it. She wished her father was there. The best years of her life were those years when he was next to her. She finally realized that it was him behind all the great results. Her alone she had failed to gather momentum. One day she remembered the last day they left the USA. Her papa had sent her back into the lab to take some stuff and among the staff, there were diaries with notes. She couldn't figure out what had happened to the notes. That night they arrived, they first went to his friend and then he left alone heading to the hotel. Leaving her with his friend. She went back to meet her papa's friend.

Andrei was older than his papa. He was like her papa's mentor growing up. She came to understand that some little things he used to do can be attributed to Andrei. She saw her papa in him. It was quite a good experience after his death. Andrei was getting older, but he remembered most of the things. They had dinner together and later that night Faye asked if her papa left some of his stuff with him. Andrei got up and went into the indoor garage and came back with a bag. He opened the bag and took out diaries and photo albums. He gave these to Faye. Tears ran down her cheeks at the sight of the photos in the album. She sobbed for some time. Later she started flicking through the diaries. She couldn't stop smiling. She looked at one of the chromosome makeup and frowns.

"Twenty-five years."

"What twenty-five years?" asked Andrei

"Can you believe it? Papa made a strain that will last for 25 years for the person who ended up betraying him."

"Can you break the chromosome code?" asked

Andrei.

"The code used by papa is unbreakable. This was applied in three phases. Most of the genetic codes are just a single jab formula and easily reversed before a certain period. The three-code application can't be reversed. The fist jab introduced the vehicles of change; that is the agents. After that, the second jab can only be applied if there is a reaction. This is because the second jab attaches only to the antibodies for it to work. The third jab then uses the antibodies to start chromosomal change. The whole process can last up to a year and we don't have that time."

"Your father was in love with this woman you know. I have never seen a man so crazy about a woman. He nearly got me run over by a car."

"Really what happened?" asked Faye.

"The first time he saw her we were in town. We were young. We were crossing the road together, but he stopped and looked at this gorgeous woman. Suddenly, he ran after the woman. I was busy checking for traffic. He was by my side, so I proceeded halfway I looked on my side and he was gone. I thought that maybe he had been hit by a car. I lost focus and panicked. I looked around that's when I saw him strolling down the road with this woman. Suddenly, a car came from nowhere and clipped my shoulder in front of oncoming traffic. The driver swerved missing me by inches before hitting a car parked nearby."

"Waal, so that was something."

"So, that explained why he made such an irreversible formula."

"There is nothing you can do. But somehow if it wasn't for her you would not be here."

"How is that so?" asked Faye.

"She refused to have kids. She chose the limelight.

Your father wanted a baby, and they always quarreled about this. One day she just woke up and left. Your father searched for her everywhere. She was gone. Then started the drinking."

"So, what about my mum? How did they meet? He never talked about it."

"Your mum was my girlfriend. We had just met nothing had happened between us. I felt sorry for him after Aija left. I was scared he would kill himself. So, I let her take him out just to give him hope, but one thing led to another. I lost both for some time. She had gone through something similar and that cemented their relationship. But every time he would talk about Aija that used to piss her off. When Aija was in town, they would break up. When she is gone, then they get back together. Your mother got fed up. After I married my childhood sweetheart after meeting at a reunion, your mother left. We never saw her again. Years later your father went looking for your mother when Aija got married and that's when he brought you. I understand she was happily married too."

Faye looked upset.

"So, she just did not get my father killed, she ruined my mum's life too? I think I know what to do," said Faye.

"What do you mean? Don't let me regret telling you this. Don't do anything stupid."

CHAPTER SEVEN

Professor Zunis entered the Vice President's office and sat down. He removed his reading glasses and blew warm breath from his mouth before wiping the glasses with his tie. He raised the glasses and looked at them before putting them back.

"Yes, professor, I want an update on the progress so far. I can tell you that the project is a great stride toward world dominance. I now have trillions of clients worldwide. Soon I will be in power. In fact, I am the one ruling."

"The professor smiled. I never thought I could be this rich."

The two had been very close over the years.

"Yes, the results. We have a list of those jabs that are about to expire, and their death partners have already been identified and located worldwide. We checked the list it appears that for 30% of them we can make more money now than to wait 10 years on average," said the professor.

"What are you saying, professor?"

The professor leans forward.

"30% of the people owe us more than 75% of the lifetime cost of the jab. It takes ten years on average to pay the full amount for the jab. But if we let nature take its course. I mean if we don't eliminate their death partners. We can double the money and get the money now rather than wait for ten years on average."

"How is that?"

"OK, the dead partner's jabs will expire at the same time, but they don't know that. They revert to their original chromosome makeup. Nature takes its toll. Or we give them a hand. They both die. No one will attribute this to the expiry of the jab because no one knows that the jabs can expire. They still must pay for the jab. But in this case, the insurance comes in. All their death policies paid off. All people owed get their share first the rest goes to the remaining family. That doubles your returns."

"I am accountable to many. I don't want to be greedy and lose everything."

"We will put countermeasures. A cleaning up operation. Whenever they die, we send our own men to do the cleaning-up. No one will know that the jabs have expired. We get paid in a year more than we are getting now. We have the funds all you need to do is to establish our own cleaning company."

"That sounds tempting."

"You want to dominate the world? Then take my advice. When the jabs expire, don't eliminate any of the death partners let both die."

"What if people ask why people have started dying?"

"We are all different, in some people the jabs take time to work, in others, they react differently. Identify a certain group of people, target those with huge pockets and say these people require an extra jab after a certain time frame. Start collecting more fees on top of what we are getting. If you do that Vice President, I will know you are serious about dominating the world. You have so much power now that any scandal will evaporate like the morning mist."

"I think I have one problem I have to take care of first before I embark on this expedition," said the Vice President.

Miles away in Russia Faye is in the lab. She looked at the pictures of her papa and her mama and cried. She went outside and started smoking. A cat came to her. She kneeled and rubbed its fur before picking up the cat. The cat looked at her and scratched her cheek. She quickly threw the cat down before cursing.

"Stupid cat. Look what you've done to me."

She looked for something in her pocket to wipe the blood but couldn't find anything. She smudges the cigarette butt and went back to the building straight to the bathroom. She looked in the mirror. And before wiping the blood she looked at herself. Suddenly her face lightens up. She left the blood flowing down her cheek until it dropped into the sink basin. She wiped the blood and walked back into the lab. She took her father's diaries and started analyzing the formulas.

Weeks passed-by, having sleepless nights working on the formula. Romero phoned her to check up on her. She quickly thought of a brilliant idea. She opened her safe where she kept all her samples and took out Romero's samples. She analyzed the samples.

"Oh, my God."

She realized that the formula was her papa's; the first version that lasted between six months to one year. After that, the chromosomes revert to their original makeup. She started researching the details of all the people who were given the jabs more than a year ago. She got the list and phoned Romero. She gave him local addresses of everyone who had been given the jab in the last years and sends Romero on a fact-finding mission to check if they are still alive or not.

Later.

"So, what did you find Romero?"

"You won't believe this. More than half of the people on the list had died within two years. Of the remaining, 10% had received a second jab. The others have either relocated or disappeared."

"Makes no sense. What is the real reason behind this? Why risk a scandal by letting all those people die?"

"I checked the autopsy reports for most of their systems reacted badly to the jab."

"Oh, I see, that's a clever one," replied Faye.

She walked up and down the lab.

"Can I ask why you took my sample? What did you find out?"

"That's not important. When did you have, yours done?"

"Hm, let's see. This month it will be nearly eleven months ago."

Faye stopped and looked at Romero with a frightened face.

"Why do you look at me like that? As if you have seen a ghost. Am I in danger?"

"No, you will be fine I guess I have to make you a new one before it runs out?" Said Faye.

"What runs out? Do you mean the jab? This is forever? Guaranteed you think I will pay thousands of dollars for something that does not last even a year. Do I look like I am crazy to you?"

"You said that the insurance company pays the money, yes?"

"In my case, no, I paid a deposit and the rest they deduct from my wages as monthly installments for the next 25 years."

"So, Romero, you owe them money for the next 25 years of your life. What incentive do they have? OK let's see; fake jab, easy money for a quarter of a century unless…"

"Unless what, Faye?"

"I need to look at that list again. Let me see half of those who died how did they pay for their jab?"

"Waal, all of them paid only the deposit, and they still owe a lot. OK if they die what will happen? Hm, let's see. The company pays their loved ones a lump sum but only after the creditors are paid first. So instead of waiting for 25 years, they get their full amount in less than 2 years. Oh! my God. I think you are in danger."

"Me in danger why? You said that you can make me another jab?"

"I know Romero. But it's of no use. They might still come for. It's not about just the jab. There is more to it. You are collateral. I think you should go and hide. I will give you another jab. But they might still send someone to clean-up."

After that day, relentlessly Faye tried to recreate the formula. After weeks of trying, she finale managed to recreate the formula. She called Andrei over. They had dinner together, and she got up and opened her papa's favorite bottle of wine. She brought two glasses and sat done.

"To Viktovha!"

"If my papa was alive today, he would be the richest and most important man in the world," said Faye raising her glass.

"He is rich, he has you. Look at me I never wanted kids. Look, I will die on my own without anyone to call my child."

"You have me, we have each other."

"That's true. You could have been my child."

"To honor my father, I want to ask you for a favor."

"Yes, what is it?"

"I have been working all the past weeks. I have managed to recreate the formula using the notes you gave me, thanks to you and my wise papa. Will you do the honors match me to her so that I can revenge my papa?"

Andrei on hearing this even though he was happy that she had managed to recreate the formula on her own, the thought of her dying made him feel very sad. He had found comfort in her. This he took very badly.

"Waste your life for that? That's not worth it. Let bygones be bygones. You have a whole life ahead of you. You can create your own jabs and start your own business."

"With her around, that will never happen. They rather have me dead than let me jeopardize her plans. By now she might have figured out that now I know."

"Administer the jabs one after the other. I have made an antidote and I have already taken this to counteract the adverse effects. To papa the great

Viktovha."

"To my dearest friend Viktovha."

The Vice President is addressing a crowd that had gathered outside her residence. One of the reporters asked a question.

"Vice President is that true that the jabs don't work at all in some people and having said that, would it be fair to refund those who find the jab useless in the light of the rising deaths."

The Vice President looked into the camera and took a big breath.

"I would like to emphasize that the jabs do work and that they will work for more than 25 years. However, having said that, in very rare cases and in certain people the person's system rejects the jab resulting in deaths. It is my understanding that my team is working tirelessly to correct that. To answer your question, we can also give those affected a second jab at a fraction of the cost. What I don't want to promise you today is to tell you that there is nothing that can be done. I don't want to go back to those days when people were helpless and hopeless when faced with the so-called death partners. Trust me, I have walked that road myself. Anyone who suggests otherwise does not know what he or she is talking about. Let's move forward with the times and not let fear undermine the great work already achieved. Thank you.”

The vice presidents started walking away. A lot of people gave applause, but some news crew people chased after her trying to ask further questions, but her bodyguards restricted them.

“Bravo that was brilliant. That’s all you had to say Mrs. Vice President that will send the money rolling in. A new phase. The second jab era. If those who don’t think they are covered enough will get the second jab as a guarantee. Now you are talking.”

The Vice President smiled and walked back into the building.

“You can start the cleaning-up now,” said professor Zunis.

Andrei walked back into the lab breathing heavily. Faye is weak and is laying on the bed. She opened her eyes and saw a shadow that resembled Andrei’s.

“You are back already; I didn’t expect you until later in the evening.” “It’s Romero.”

“What about him?”

“He was found dead today. Gunshot he didn’t stand a chance. In broad daylight to make things worse.”

“Any clues as to who is behind this?”

"A formidable force. One we don't want to mess up with we have a big schedule ahead of us. From now, we have to go to my place and finish everything there."

"We need all this equipment. I will come back and do the remainder but for you, it's not safe anymore."

Faye struggled to get up. The jabs were making her very weak. She had weeks to nurse the side effects before the new change takes effect. They took whatever they were after and left the building. Faye started crying in the back seat. Andrei pulled the car on the road shoulders.

"What seems to be the matter? I thought we were doing fine."

Faye kept sobbing for a while before she replied.

"I remember the last day we left the USA, like yesterday. It was such a traumatic experience for me. I was young. It is one of the times I really bonded with my father. We were close. Ever since he came to take me. I was his princess."

"You still are."

The following day Andrei was back in the lab going through some formulas. He kept trying to make formulas with the help of the computer but after a while the formula scrambles. He tried different combinations but still, the result was the same. The formula in the end destabilized.

"This was my formula Viktovha developed and advanced. Where am I going wrong?" Andrei spoke to himself in the lab. He took a jab and shoots himself after sterilizing everything. He gave himself two more jabs and slumped on the bed in the other room in the lab.

He woke up feeling very sick. He called for a cab and left the building heading to his place.

Faye was feeling better now but still weak.

"Andrei, what happened to you?"

"I guess, a sign of old age. I am getting weak and weak. I prepared the final jab for your formula. I can administer it now."

After a while, Faye received the last jab. She was happy at least she was going to put an end to all this.

Professor Zunis knocked at the Vice President's door. She was in her office with a delegate of potential investors into her new adventure.

"I am kind of busy now. Can you come back later

professor?"

The Vice President resumed talking to her delegates. The professor remained standing there. One of the delegates pointed to the Vice President to the presence of the professor.

"Professor I said I can't talk right now. I am in the middle of something."

"I am afraid this can't wait."

"What is it professor why you show me no respect in front of my clients. I am afraid there is something you must see. Come with me."

The Vice President looked at her delegates and excused herself.

"Enjoy the refreshments I will be with you soon."

The Vice President and the professor walked through several doors until they reached the lab. The professor quickly brought up a screen with some chromosome formula.

"So, what is this?"

"I just received this from our office in Russia. One of the subjects has part of your formula."

"That cheeky spoiled brat. I should have trusted my

instincts and got rid of her. See what happens if I put emotions in what I do."

"Don't bit up yourself. Her father bribed you with some twenty-five years guaranteed formula. I could have done the same myself but that's not important right now. The big question is how much did she know, and she is capable of reproducing the formula?"

"But I thought you said that's part of the formula."

"Yes, I guess this was just a free jab. I am just saying that if someone is prepared to pay huge sums can she reproduce the formula?"

"As far as I know never. She was just a little girl the time they left. Unless… that bastard is giving her a hand… I think we should send the cleaners there."

"Which bastard? Where, Mrs. Vice President?"

Days after Andrei invited his old friend over. They had a good time and Andrei pleaded with him to stay and look after his house while they were on vacation. He was happy to accept. One morning Andrei and Faye packed their bags and left, leaving Zimmer home. A car arrived outside Andrei's house and a stronghold of six men got out of the car and surrounded the place. Two entered the building. Zimmer had been drinking vodka and was slumped on the couch the time they arrived. He heard the noise and opened his eyes. He got up to see clearly what was going on.

"Who is that? Is that you?"

Zimmer didn't finish speaking before a bullet lodged in his brain. The men swiftly moved in. They collected the samples and stuffed the man in the deep freezer after taking all the reindeer meat out.

The men left the place.

Faye and Andrei are seated in the woods near a lake. It's frozen everywhere. Andrei goes in the woods to fetch some wood. He brought the wood and started the fire.

"You set up the fires before you even caught the fish. Isn't that a little strange?"

"You tell me?"

"What do you mean? You lost me."

"I know all your plans. You are just like your father, calculating and manipulative. Don't be a smart ass."

"If you were in my shoes you would understand?"

"We talked about this it's not worth dying for. Let it go. You have your whole life ahead of you."

"I don't know about you, but I can't be a sitting duck. I would rather decide how it will end than some greedy person to dictate how I should live my life."

"You are stubborn just like your father. You can start your own company. Challenge them to prove you are better and more worth it than them then the world will be on your side."

"You know that's just fancy talk. These people are bad people. Yeah, you trying to be clever you are just like my papa too. I am not a kid anymore you know." "What do you mean?"

"You know that right now, she is after you too. You let your best friend die for you?"

"Zimmer has no one. If it wasn't for you, I could have stayed there. You gave me hope, a daughter I had never had. It hurts to think that at one point in my life I had the chance to have a beautiful daughter or son only to be robbed four months down the line."

"How come you never talked about it?"

"Faye, some things are better left in the past? I think you are a coward just like your father. Giving up, choosing rather to die than to fight."

"I don't know what you are talking about."

"I was not born yesterday. If I knew that you were just going to recreate your father's formula, I was not going to give you the notes. Why not make your own and stop embarrassing your father? You think he just died so that you die too. I think he gave you a chance to prove that all those years when he was not there you were doing fine. He regretted taking you from your mother. He is a bad influence. Look, speeding toward self-destruction. See what separates me from you. I let others, wear my shoes and feel the pain. Sometimes to do nothing is actually to do all."

"There is no other option you know it's only a matter of time before she sends someone."

Professor Zunis is in the lab when his cell phone rang.

"Dimitri speaking."

"Professor I have just sent you a report on our latest subject please check the report straight away."

"OK, just hold on I download the attachment," he looked at the file.

"Are you sure about this? That can't be right."

"I thought so myself. I have sent you the original

sample analyze it yourself it will arrive tonight."

The professor sits down and analyzed the file and chromosome composition.

"Damn! We are in trouble."

"What is it Zunis?"

"We are in deep trouble. The Vice President is going to ask for our heads on a plate. Someone out there can recreate her formula. I told her that it was hard to recreate. I failed many times to recreate it. This person has created two of the jabs. Once he created the last jab, then the Vice President will be no more. Honestly, I think this should stay among us. I need time to find a way to alter her formula and compositional structure."

Over the party, the professor is talking to the Vice President.

"I received news today that the subject was taken down."

"How did it happen and where was he?"

"Cornered at home and shot in the head they are analyzing his samples as we speak?"

"Cornered at home? Are you sure?"

The Vice President looked confused and unconvinced.

"You mean, cornered at his home. The address I have given you?"

"Correct, Vice President."

"There must be something wrong."

"What do you mean Vice President?"

"He is not the type of person you can corner at home, let alone kill in cold blood. I want to see the samples and ask them to take photos. Leave the body in the freezer. I will need it."

"Okay, Mrs. Vice President. Will do that."

For the first time, the professor looked worried and fear was written all over his face. The Vice President knew he was not being honest with her.

Later that day she took out her phone and phoned her Moscow branch.

"Professor can I see you in my office straight away."

The professor after receiving the call went into the bathroom. He looked at himself in the mirror and poured cold water on his face. He reached for the bathroom towel and dosed his face. He walked out and headed to the Vice President's office. His ankles were literally trembling. He knocked on the door and minutes later a voice answered asking him to come in. There was a laptop on the desk with a picture of the chromosome formula, the one he was hiding.

"We have been working together for a very long time I expect more from you. I hate hearing this from Moscow when you are a block downstairs. Now. Can you explain what is going on?"

The professor took off his reading glasses and looked at the Vice President.

"Yes, go on. Is something wrong?"

"I don't know how to say this Mrs. Vice President. We have a problem."

He paused and looked outside the window for a while, this time the Vice President remained quiet.

"We have another subject, presumably with two jabs of your formula. When I got the files, honestly I panicked especially when I knew what all this means."

"What does this mean professor?" asked the Vice President sitting up straight.

"Someone is creating a time bomb for you. It's only a matter of time. I am short of words; I don't know what to tell you, but we can't crack the formula."

"What are you saying? Suicide death partner? Really who? You said that they killed Andrei. Then who?"

"Honestly I don't know. I was going to ask you that question. Who in your past is capable of doing that?"

"Professor as far as I know only Andrei had the guts to do that unless…."

Quickly the Vice President got up and stood near the window facing outside. She touched her chin before coming back to sit down. She reached for the phone and requested a secure line.

"Moscow office please."

She showed the professor her left-hand index finger and waited to be connected to the Moscow office.

They heard the phone ringing on the other side. Minutes later someone answered the phone.

"Halo" How can I help you?"

"I requested photos of the subject. I want them now.

Can you fax them straight away? This can't wait."

"OK check your fax machine straight away."

The Vice President quickly placed the receiver down and looked at the professor before she breathed heavily.

"So, professor, what can we do to be prepared for this?"

"I wanted to find out more about this before I discussed this with you. So far, it's just speculative. There might not be another person out there with the complete formula. Which is good for us? If there is, then, the question to ask is this; is there a person suicidal enough and bearing hatred toward you out there, to do something stupid?"

"Andrei, maybe, to get back at me for dumping him but that was many years ago. Viktovha is so long gone. His daughter... eh... not sure about her."

"What about his daughter? I have to know

everything if I have to help you?"

"Honestly I don't think so... I sent a lot of money many years ago, to her. Unless if this has nothing to do with money. You know what, let's get the photos first then we can talk about this. What is taking so long? Why Moscow has to keep me waiting all the time?"

They talked about something else for a while waiting for the fax papers. A beeping sound came from the fax machine and printing in progress noise is heard coming from the machine. The Vice President got up quickly and walked to the fax machine in the corner. She looked at the image as it slowly came from the fax machine. Just after a fraction of the image is printed the Vice President cursed.

"Damn! I knew it. That bastard is still alive somewhere out there. Find him! And kill him! I want him dead! He can't ruin my plans. Why am I paying these people for? What must I do to get things done around here?"

The Vice President shouted with a harsh angry voice. Red-faced, her eyes red with anger hitting the table sending the papers flying. The professor kneeled to pick up the image just sent from Moscow. He looked at the Vice President and saw nothing than rage.

"So at least we know who is behind this."

"I knew it. He is still alive. Maybe I have to go there myself."

"Very risk Vice President. If he has your formula, the outcome can be unpredictable."

"Then do something! Don't just sit there get to work! I want him stopped! No, no, no. I can't let him ruin my plans."

The professor got up and quickly left the office going back to the lab.

The Vice President walked to the window and stood there looking outside. She opened the cabinet and took out a small box. She opened it and took an old photo out mounted on a frame. She sat down. She looked at the picture and smiled for a while.

"Son of a…… (hitting the table very hard). I should have killed you when I had the chance."

She sat down comfortably resting her back on the sofa and placed her hands together after placing the picture on her desk. In the picture, three people are in the boat. She is surrounded by two men. She looked very happy, and the photo is signed and has the words; always forever. The Vice President picked up the phone and called a number after requesting a secure line.

The person on the other end picked up the phone. The Vice President spoke in the Russian language.

"Hello, my friend. It has been a long time. I have a job for you. Operation Always Forever."

"Are you sure? I thought you and...."

"Yes. I know, but that was a long time ago. Can you do it?"

A private small plane glides over an icy frozen lake. A man with only boxer shorts is walking on top of the frozen river barefooted as the plane passed-by. Hot steam is coming out of his mouth. He walked across the frozen river until he reached the other side. He picked up a slashing blade and walked on top of the river. He looked down through the iced water. He smiled. A golden orange fish surfaced and can be seen just under the ice kissing the ice on top. He walked close to the bank of the frozen river. He stabbed the icy water and started cutting the ice. He cuts a small square block and the ice block fell into the water. Soon after A golden orange fish rushed to the opening but soon disappeared at the sight of the man. The man jumped into the icy waters and resurfaced soon afterward. He got out and pushed his hair backward. He walked to the bank and sat down preparing to set up the fire. A distance away a reindeer appeared from nowhere and looked at the man. The eyes of the man and the animal met, and instincts kicked in, as the reindeer retreated. Soon after it stopped a few feet away and started chewing the leaves that were in its mouth. The man slowly smiled and picked up his rifle. He kneeled and took aim at the reindeer.

CHAPTER EIGHT

The man's hand slowly reached for the trigger. Suddenly a fish jumped out of the water and flipped up and down, side to side gasping for air. That distracted the man who fired a shot, anyway, missing the reindeer. The noise startled the reindeer. Instantly it ran for its life and disappeared into the surrounding woods. The man looked at the fish and smiled. He picked up the slashing blade and stabbed the fish lifting it up before walking to the fire. He sat down. Another fish jumped out of the water and flipped up and down. Somehow before the man picked it up, the fish found its way back into the water. The man had already stood up. He looked down only to find that the fish had already gone. He found it funny that he laughed and sat back down.

He grilled the fish. Minutes later the man enjoyed the roasted fish. After that, he searched his bag and took out a bottle of vodka. He drank it for a while before he squinted his face and gave a big burp. He closed the bottle and placed the bottle on his side. The man is Yugosnki, an ex KGB, a ruthless experienced assassin. After the collapse of the KGB, he had worked as an assassin.

Later he is driving his car and after a while, he arrived at a house in Moscow. He carried a small bag into the house. He sat in the sitting room. He checked messages on the answerphone. There was one message. He listened to the message and after the message, he picked up the phone and dialed a number. He spoke in the Russian language. After a while he got a bottle of whiskey from the cabinet and sat down. He watched the news. He started dozing off on the couch and the sound of the doorbell ringing woke him up. He got up and walked to the door. Firstly, he checked his handgun before peeping through the small glass hole on the door. He unlocked the door, and a man looked left and right before quickly getting into the house. He sat in the sitting room. Minutes later he got up and poured the whiskey. He brought a bag and left this on the table. "Did you bring all the stuff I asked you to bring?"

"Everything, in there," said Yanka pointing at the bag.

"I can go with you if you want just like the KGB days, but you give me 50% of what you get."

Yugosnki poured all the contents of the glass in his mouth before replying.

"30% only just because you are my friend, otherwise I can do it by myself, easy, and for old time sake. What do you say?"

"40% I can do with some cash right now my friend."

"OK, 40%."

The two men spoke for a very long time before Yanka left.

Sammy is sat on a swinging chair at his desk analyzing the woman's chromosome and blood samples. He looked at the report. He swung and looked at Nancy. He looked at the report again.

"You won't believe the results. She was rejuvenating. Her cells were growing and dividing as in youth. For some reason, the telomeres were growing in length. They were both old. I would have expected something like this is we have used the specimen of youth and that of an old person. In other words, life can be recycled. The process can be restarted again."

"Sammy, are you saying that she was getting young again?"

"Not necessarily but I am saying that the body can regrow or rejuvenates, the skin can be smooth again the wrinkles can disappear again naturally. Gray hairs can give way to new colored hairs. Life can be prolonged, for how long? I don't know but I am saying this is possible. The greatest achievement, which is the key, I think is the regrowth of the telomeres. These in normal circumstances determine whether the cells rejuvenate and grows or shrinks and become inactive. For the first time, I have witnessed their growth. This will eliminate aging as all cells will continue to grow and rejuvenates," said Sammy.

"I think there is still a lot we don't know. Let's try to find out why people age? Why rejuvenation stops? Why bodies will be weak and unable to eliminate diseases once one gets old. I think a thorough analysis of the first and second samples might shed light on this."

"I have been collecting samples of all fluids and breath which I condensed and refrigerated. Concentrations of certain molecules decreases with time with the highest concentrations in the first samples," said Sammy.

"So how can that shade light on regrowth and rejuvenation?" asked Nancy.

Sammy sits up straight and looked at Nancy.

"This is how I see things. Let's say in the beginning we have a vital molecule in our body and initial concentration is high. But we as humans we take and excrete fluids depending on our habits. This molecule is vital for our body and is easily affected by the amounts of fluids we take in our body. So, in the long run, the amount that will be left in our body will depend on the amount of fluid intake and how much of this molecule we lose. If this molecule is vital for our survival and we keep on losing some in urine and vapor, then when it depletes our bodies will stop growing. Are you with me?" asked Sammy.

"Go on I am listening," replied Nancy.

"When the molecule depletes in our body as we excreted it, then after a certain number of years this molecule will be finished, and our bodies will stop functioning properly. In the end, death will be eminent. So, having said that. I think these people in the last days, they look for their chromosome twins for them to initiate rejuvenation all this is attributed to survival instincts."

"Sammy, but how can they change the chromosome without any medical procedure? In all cases, they just locked themselves in a single room only to be found dead the following day."

"That's something that has been giving me sleepless nights. After looking at all the cases, I personally think that, and this is just my own view. I think whatever it is that sustains life. It is lost in the breath. Breath is the key. When a person dies, he loses breath. So, life is in the breath. Whatever causes people to die is in the breath. Whatever we lose is in the breath."

"That really makes sense," said Nancy.

"So, my first assumption is that. We lose vital elements by breathing them out. It's nothing to do with water that is lost through urine or sweat. It's strictly through the air we breathe. We lose life elements or molecules through breath. We lose elements responsible for growth and rejuvenation through breath. We lose aging fighting elements or molecules through breath. Are you with me Nancy?"

"Go on Sammy. I am listening to."

"OK, my second assumption is that life-supporting elements are breathed out as vapor in the breath. So,

I am saying. Vital molecules or elements are dissolved in liquids but most escapes as vapor and are breathed out. Few quantities escape in the urine or sweat glands. I think these people know that. Why do they come together, lock the rooms they are in and close all the windows? To avoid air escaping. Two people together with the same chromosome make-up are likely to emit the same elements out. So, they benefit by emitting the same elements and at the same time reabsorbing the elements in large quantities, thereby exchanging or enhancing the missing elements to restart rejuvenation."

"That's very clever, that will answer all the cases even where a small child was involved," added Nancy.

"Exactly. Although the composition is the same, we are all different, you might emit one element more than the other person. So, coming together tends to let one absorb one element he is missing and at the end that tends to balance back the elements and initiate rejuvenation," said Sammy.

"So, Sammy I have looked at all cases involving an adult and a young person. In all cases, the element balance of the older was way depleted and required enormous replacement."

"That's correct. Like I said at first, we have more of these elements when we are young. I think also that our bodies can replace these elements when we are young than when we are old. So, I am saying that in theory, if we have two people with the same chromosome makeup. One very old and the other young we can rejuvenate the old one using the breath of the young person. We can replenish the molecules and elements responsible for growth and

rejuvenation. We can stop or even reverse aging."

"Sammy, I think that makes sense. That is the only hypothesis that explains all the cases so far. These people are not gathering randomly. Instincts, nature knows that this is the way to cheat death."

"Open our domain for our website and it should be www. breathbanks.com. Register our company by that name also, with the money we have we should start offering services for people to come and deposit their breath at regular intervals from an earlier age. When they are old, we will give them their own breath to restart cell rejuvenation. In the long run, you and me, we will be the pioneers of everlasting life. Wrinkles and old age will be a thing of the past. Mankind shall live forever or for hundreds of years in their youthful state. And if it pleases you, I would be happy to call you Mrs. Nancy Plivdasnki," said Sammy kneeling on one knee.

"Ah, Sammy, I will be honored I thought you never ask," said Nancy leaning forward to kiss Sammy.

"Mr. Sammy and Mrs. Nancy Plivdasnki the first to discover longevity."

Applause.

"Sammy, the following will be our slogan."

"Don't breathe your life away! Deposit your breath today. Contact Breathbank and start saving your life today."

"That's why I love you, I can't figure out why it took me so long to tell you this. I love you, Nancy."

Nancy is four months pregnant, and she walked toward the big office windows. She leaned out the window rubbing her belly with her right hand. She looked outside as a car entered the parking space in front of the office. A man well-dressed in a suit-wearing glasses jumped out of the car and looked at Nancy. He waved his hand and smiled infectiously. He closed the doors and started walking toward the office. He entered the office.

"Babes, I am back. How has it been for you?"

"Great been busy the whole day people have been coming and going. Just in four months, we have over a million people. Just imagine what it will be like by the end of the year. I am afraid we will run out of storage space," said Nancy.

"Don't worry about that I have just signed a storage deal. We will acquire land to build a huge storage facility so that should not be a problem."

"Great news, guess who is one of our new subscribers? Someone powerful," said Nancy.

"The Vice President?"

"No. Why would she subscribe to our project when she has a zillion dollar-project herself?"

"I don't know. I just wish she can see our point of view. It will be great to have her on our side."

"Why? Do you want to be part of that? Something is not right with that woman. I personally think they are not telling the people the truth about the jabs. It's a shame we never found someone to prove that they really work."

"Nancy darling, so tell me, who is it?"

"The President himself."

"No way, the President? Isn't he on the same footing as the Vice President?"

"Ask him yourself after lunch Sammy."

"What do you mean? He is coming here. Waal, I never dreamed that he would buy that. Wait a minute, does that mean the jabs are not working, or he just wants both best worlds? I guess I must ask him that. So, let's go for lunch darling."

Later in the afternoon the President arrived with his bodyguards in secrecy and met Sammy and his wife Nancy. After depositing his own breath, they entered the office.

"So, young man, you are the brains behind all this? I personally think it's a good idea. It makes sense and there are no side effects and it's not that expensive and risky than the jabs?" said the President.

"Best of both worlds should I say?" asked Sammy.

"The President looked around and leaned forward. Me jabs? No. I want natural things. You can call me old fashion if you like. I have been here for a long time. I have seen it all. Who would not want to live forever? But it's always good to read the small print. I don't want to sign my life away like that. Don't get me wrong. I think it's a brilliant idea but just not for me. Your idea, Fantastic. Keep up with the good work only time will tell but you have my support."

"Thank you, Mr. President."

In a village in remote Russia, there is a house covered in snow. A man came out and stood outside smoking. He looked around smoking. A lady came out too and they all stood outside smoking.

"Winters, this side is very cold," said Faye.

"It's cold everywhere but I don't mind the snow. In fact, I love snow. In winter, I am not miserable. I don't worry too much. Everyone is happy. I have a very good excuse to drink whenever I like. Vodka keeps me warm and happy."

"So, will they not come here looking for us?"

"Maybe, but I think it will take time for them to figure out that I am here. I used to come here a lot, me and your papa. Good memories. Very good place to wind down and reflect on things. You know?"

"I don't know how this will end but I would like you to have this." Andrei draws a handgun and aimed far away first before giving it to Faye. She placed the cigarette between her lips and took the gun. She squints one eye and spoke with the cigarette in her mouth.

"I never used one before. You are going to show me how to use it right?"

"Yes, it is easy to use. If you want to wear warm clothes. We go for a walk."

Quickly Faye threw the cigarette in the snow on the ground and entered the house. Soon after Andrei entered the house too. They both left and headed in the woods nearby. They started practicing. At first, Faye struggled and after a while, she became better and better.

Somewhere in the same woods a distance away two men are walking carrying satchels. They have snow boots and heavy winter clothing. They walked for a while one in front of the other following through the narrow road in the woods. The man in front who happened to be Yugosnki stopped and passed a bottle of whiskey to Yanka.

"My friend after this I want to come and settle here. I love the countryside. I love nature. City live, I can't stand. I will have my own farm with this money I want to establish myself here." They walked for a while before they heard gunshot sounds.

"Listen to that?"

"We are near, better be them."

Andrei quickly took a gadget from his pocket. The gadget was vibrating. He looked at it.

"Damn we have a company we have to go to. Come hurry let's go."

Faye and the old man ran as fast as they can go back to the house. They took whatever they needed and left.

"Keep running we have to go far away from here." They soon disappeared in the wood.

Yugosnki and Yanka arrived at the place where Faye and Andrei were practicing to shoot. Yugosnki kneeled and picked up the bullet shells. He looked at the size of the footprints.

"It's them. Look at the shoe sizes. The old man training that girl to shoot."

"How old is she?" asked Yanka.

"Mid-twenties. They want both alive. The man is ex KGB, it's going to take some clever moves to capture both alive. We must keep the trail fresh before it's dark."

"So, let's go"

The two men followed the footsteps, running. These led them to a house. Smoke was coming out of the house. Yugosnki pointed to the left, and he started walking toward the right. Yanka went via the left side to cover the back of the house. They limped forward slowly. Yugosnki opened the door and jumped inside taking cover on the floor. He searched all the other rooms. The house was empty, he signaled to Yanka who came inside.

"Maybe we should wait for them here where they can't go, anyway. The next place is miles away from here," said Yanka.

"Former KGB, somehow he knows we are here. We need them alive, so we have to follow them."

"Yes, former KGB but he is with the girl. She can't stand this weather".

"We better be moving before it's dark."

The pair went outside and started looking for the recent foo-steps.

"Check which ones are the recent ones. Go that way and let me know if you find any?"

For some time, the two-kept going around the house bending down searching for recent prints.

"Damn he knew we are coming after them. He tried to lose the trail. OK, you follow that path after twenty minutes come back, we meet here. Check if it's the correct path."

The two men separated and disappeared.

Andrei and Faye are running away, and Faye is breathing very fast, occasionally looking back.

"Don't stop. Keep running we must cover a long distance before it's dark. The next house if a bit far."

"I am very tired. I need to rest for a while."

She bends holding her knees breathing heavily.

"Be strong, young lady. I am an old man look at me you should be ahead of me."

"Andrei, I have run for a long time. Somehow I am quickly getting tired."

"She will only send the best. Trust me you don't want to be near these guys. Pull yourself up and let's go."

The two started running in the woods. After a while, Faye screamed and ran in a different direction.

Andrei stopped and pointed the gun at the bear.

"It's just a bear keep moving it's not like it's going to attack us. This is its territory so like I said keep moving."

By the time they reached the other house, it was dark. Faye wanted just to lay down and sleep. She smiled when she saw the house. There were lights in the house. At last the comfort of a house and warm food. They had left all the tinned food in the other house.

"Why are you smiling?"

"My legs are sore, and I am exhausted, I think we should stay here for the night."

"Stay here? Are you out of your mind? These people will kill all of us if we stay."

"So, what will stop them?"

"Let's just say I sent them a powerful message. That will guarantee your safety."

"So, why we came here?"

“We need a car. If you are not brave enough, I suggest you stay outside here.” “Brave Enough for what?”

“We need a car, right?”

“So?”

“Stop acting like a kid. Do you think they will just give us the car? Okay, you know what? You stay here. Keep this. If anything happens, run that way as fast as you can and ask for help.”

“Andrei, are you going to kill them?”

“If I have to? I am going to assume that they will cooperate. Do you have any money with you maybe try to negotiate first?”

“Yes.”

Faye took notes from her wallet and gave these to Andrei.

“OK, you wait here. If I am not out in twenty minutes run as fast you can in that direction okay?” Faye nodded her head.

Andrei proceeded toward the house carrying a gun. His heart beating very fast. Minutes passed before Andrei returned. Faye looked around and saw a horse. She slowly started going there. She reached the shade and peeped inside. She saw a land-rover car inside. She opened the shade and entered inside. The car was locked. A horse that was inside startled her sending her jumping, ending up on the ground. The horse made noises. A few seconds later she heard a gunshot sound. Fear crippled her; she ran toward the house. She reached the door and carefully slides the door open. The man is shot, and he is touching his shoulder sitting on the floor. The woman is beside him. The look on their faces said it all.

"Where is your car? Give me the keys before I shot you?"

"The car is in the shade, Andrei."

"What are you doing here? I told you to wait for me outside. It's not even twenty minutes. Why do you call me by my name? See now you left me with no option. I have to smoke them"

"Give me the bloody keys to the land-rover in the shade or I will shoot you all." Shouted Faye shaking her hands uncontrollably aiming at the man and then the wife.

"OK, OK don't shoot they are in the cabinet. Please don't shoot just take the car and go. We won't say anything."

Faye quickly got the keys and the pair quickly left the house into the shade and drove away.

"Quick thinking, but do as I tell you. If you stayed where you were there was no need to shoot them. They were going to give me the keys after twenty minutes."

"Really? They looked like they were not going to cooperate," said Faye.

"Dead people are the best co-operators."

Faye looked at Andrei as they drove away from the woods.

The Vice President is talking to people as they are at a meeting. Minutes later they are outside a garden shade having drinks.

"Great speech Vice President. This year is your year to shine."

"Has been already. Thanks, and will continue to do so, am I correct?"

"Depends on what you are going to do and which course of action you will take."

"Okay, what is going on?"

"This is unofficial, but rumors have it that the

President deposited in his breath in the Breathbank?"

"What Breathbank?"

"Someone in the city established a Breathbank. It's an alternative to what you are offering, at a reduced price and I think people are buying the idea."

"Why no one said anything about this to me?"

"I didn't know I only find out myself recently."

"Find out what you know about that person. I want to know all his background information. I want to know his sources of income. His family and how he is doing? I want to know any information they have that tends to undermine my business. I want that information on my desk by the end of today?"

"Can you arrange an appoint for me to see the President?" said the Vice President.

Days later, the President is talking to the Vice President.

"It's funny I never heard you again regarding the jabs despite you promising me that you will come and get a jab, Mr. President."

"Just been too busy. These things are complicated for me. I am old fashioned I want straight forward things."

"So, are you saying that Breathbank is better than my company?"

"It's simple to understand. I like the idea. I just go there and give them my breath. I don't get anything. I am giving and I am not getting. That alone gives me peace of mind. I don't have to worry if something goes wrong after a year or so."

"I thought your life should matter more. That person you are endorsing, swindled money from the government do you know that?"

The Vice President took out an envelope with photos taken when the President visited the Breathbank and placed these on the desk.

"That does not mean anything do you have proof that he swindled money from the government?"

The Vice President smiled and walked to the window. She looked outside for some time. It's not just about embezzling funds. That person also kidnapped a woman and experimented with her until the day she died. They killed her. Shall I go on?" asked the Vice President handing over the photos of the woman the day she died.

"That can't be right. I asked my man to check on him they said he is clean."

"You believe anyone, Mr. President. You refused to trust me, so I won't trust you too."

"I haven't broken any rules by the way. Whatever I went for was personal."

"You expressed poor judgment. You are the leader of the people and you should lead by example."

The President got up and walked to the window. He looked nervous though but not frightened. The Vice President smiled with every move squeezing him in the corner ready to strike. At last this man was going down faster and sooner than she had hoped for.

"You said that he embezzled funds? How? Was he in the government before?"

"Mr. President, there are a lot of things you don't know. I personally think you made a huge judgmental error and because of that I will make sure that people will see it from my point of view that you are unfit to run the country."

"You have all the power and money you need what more do you want?"

"No, you still have the power. My power is not endorsed by congress. I want people to see who you truly are."

"We will see, there are a lot of things you have been hiding from me too. All the unexplained deaths and all lump-sum payments by insurance companies what are they for?"

"To be honest, if I were you, I would not go that road"

"So why talk about my mistakes when you have got a log in your eye?"

"I am talking to you as a friend. Years back we found out that government money was being embezzled. I personally set up a task force to investigate this." "Without my approval? I am the President."

"Listen first."

The Vice President leans forward.

"This task force found out that there was someone blackmailing Senator Roy. This person got the senator's chromosome composition and engineered a perfect copy in the lab." She paused and looked outside for a while after breathing heavily.

"Yes, go on."

"The Senator fearing for his life, which is understandable, paid millions of government money to a one Sammy Plivdasnki. This same person who used to run a lab in the city. So, this Sammy used genetically engineered viruses to create a perfect match for the Senator. He blackmailed him. The Senator after paying him millions of government money was killed by this Sammy."

"Damn, what did I get myself into? Are you sure about this?" asked the President.

"If it was the true death-partner of the Senator, the woman could have died too at the same time. Everyone knows that. But this conniving, manipulating young man kept the women experimenting on her until the day she died. After she died, he abandoned her there to decay until the day she was found. We are looking at embezzling funds, blackmail, blackmailing not just anyone but the Senator, causing the death of the Senator, causing the death of the woman, misrepresenting information, breaking health and safety rules in dealing with harmful organism, kidnapping the woman, experimenting on humans, breaking all the humanity acts, and now establishing a company that put the service of the public at risk without proper certification. But, to be honest, he can get away with all this if he wanted to."

"How is that so?"

"The world has changed too. You must move with the times. If he is smart enough, he can say that he was carrying out the presidential commands. That will clean him and leave the burden of proof on you. We have witnesses who have seen you together. We have these photos that show you were in contact with each other. Him, being under you he had every right to carry out whatever you asked him to do. The Senator is dead. He can simply say the Senator was acting on your behalf. Why would the government pay him millions if they didn't have a vested interest? His wife is four months pregnant. There are a lot of people out there who will sympathize with him. A lot of people end up in cases like this. How can you separate personal and official duties when they go hand in hand?"

"Damn, OK I see your point. What do you want?"

"Honestly nothing but it will be good for you to endorse my jabs firstly publicly. Secondly, you can remain in power but as a dummy President. You will take orders from me. I am not asking much, am I? Thirdly and the most important. I want you to sign a declaration that will make having my jabs compulsory by everyone, young or old. Fourthly I want you to go and talk to this Sammy. Explain that you sympathize with him and his dreams but because of the Senator's death he must leave the country if he doesn't. Then you will get him arrested. I want you to ask this young man to transfer ownership of his company to you. Then later, you will transfer ownership to me. This is what you say. The company was started with swindled government money and therefore belonged to the government. Be harsh at first but acknowledge he tried to help, given the circumstances when people were dying but that does not give him the right to kill a government official and kidnap a helpless lady only to let her die. On top of that, he deceived the President. I know he still has enough money to start a new life so take everything that doesn't offer him anything. We will recover our money from insurance for the whole family."

"What! What do you mean? You still want to tarnish my name even further huh?" asked the President.

"That's all you have to do. You are still in power inverted commas. Everyone is happy and we can cover up everything. Any scandal will damage us both. What do you say?"

The President sat in his chair without knowing what to do. This was a tough call either way. He had tough decisions to make.

"What was I thinking? I think I have no choice. I will go there today. I will pretend I was personally assessing him after all the accusations I heard."

"Good. I will get my boys ready?"

"Mind you, he is expecting a baby don't do

anything stupid?"

"It's either him or you? What do you suggest I do?" asked the Vice President.

CHAPTER NINE

Weeks after, the Vice President and the President are together at the official opening of the Breathbank company. A lot of people had gathered there, television crews and reporters were all outside. The crowd was cheering on.

"Mr. President! Leaked sources suggested that you were the first member of the government to come and deposit your breath here what do you say to that?"

"That was an official business trip to try to negotiate the takeover. Whatever projects, especially ones involved with making people live hundreds of years surely any government will want to be part of that. We are no different. They said to lead by example and I just did that. Today I am very happy and pleased to be part of this great achievement. The Breathbank company today belongs to the government. Surely, we want to be involved. I personally signed a new law today to make jabs and breath deposits compulsory."

As soon as he had announced that, the crowd went crazy everyone talking to each other.

"Don't you think that you are going too far, Mr. President? It's like telling everyone how they should live their lives," asked one reporter.

"The President looked at the reporter, the crowd and the Vice President.

"Let me make this clear to every one of you. Today I made the jabs and the breath deposits as compulsory and that is what is going to happen. I will do whatever it takes to save your lives. This is the future. There shall be no death. People shall live for hundreds of years as young as they like. I urge everyone to work with me in these tough times. To achieve this, we must be tough and committed as well. Humans will always doubt everything it's our nature and our greatest weakness. For the past two thousand years' man has been dying despite great advancement in medicine. Today genetic engineering has enabled our bodies to grow and regrow and rejuvenate. Please be patient with us but together we shall never die again."

People cheered everyone clapping hands and cheering.

"Mr. President. An investigation into the jabs highlighted inadequacies as some people suggested that they all never lasted for a year even though the money is collected for up to 25 years can you shed some light on that."

"See when we first started, no one knows what was going on. Everything was on a trial-and-error basis.

Look where is Senator Roy? This is how serious
this is. We have lost very good people and we don't
want to lose you too. To answer your question. We
are all different, for some, after one year, we found
out that they will need the second jab as the first
one weakened. We have put that in place. Today,
we realized that some people would benefit from air
therapy using their own air to deplete the lost
elements. I guarantee you that, tomorrow we will
notice some inadequacies as well but we as a
government, we are taking every step to ensure that
we will always be ready. So, let's take this
opportunity to thank the great brain behind all this,
ladies and gentlemen, Vice President Aija."

The President stepped backward, giving the floor to
the Vice President. Over recent weeks, people had
noticed that these two had become very close
together. The Vice President addressed the crowd
and answered some questions as well.

An air drone flies over a residential area. Parcels are
being left in the dropping zones in the yard. A drone
landed in a yard and left a small parcel on the lawn
of one of the houses. After a while, a girl, a little
older came out of the house and picked up the
parcel. the dog followed her back into the house.
She slumped on the couch leaving the parcel on the
table. She flicked through the television channels
and started watching entertainment channels. Her
mum came down from upstairs.

"Do you want to play our game? Get ready. Wear your magic dress."

"Mummy, I am not a two-year-old anymore. I don't want to play this silly game, okay?"

"This game is for all ages. Let's play. OK, this will be the last one."

The girl looked grumpy and bored.

"You used to love this game when you were young."

"Mum, I have played this game so many times, I lost count."

While the two were busy talking. The girls' mum was loading coordinates from a small paper she took from the magazine. The code is read and processed by the reading glasses before it is converted into audio. As the voices are played by the earphones, the points are instantly marked, pinned and flagged on the map. The girl came back.

"I don't fit this dress anymore I have grown up."

"Now I understand why you don't like this game anymore. I will buy you a new one. Are you ready? Change the channel and let's play."

"Can I play without the magic hat? It won't fit as

well?"

"Yes sure. Okay, here we go."

A beeping sound is heard on the television and the daughter aimed before taking a shot. The image turned red before the screen is clear. Another different image appeared on the same spot. The girl looked surprised and confused. She looked at her mum. Even her mum knew this was the first time two images appeared on the same sport.

"Mummy are you sure that this is correct? I have never seen two images on the same spot."

"Okay give me a second. I will try to find out what is going on."

Her mum checked everything making sure these were the correct coordinates.

"As far as I know, they are correct coordinates, let's play."

The girl threw imaginary missiles at the image. Soon after, the image appeared bloodied and disappeared soon after.

After just two imagery targets there were no more targets. The girl looked surprised even worse. For the past years, they were a minimum of five targets each session.

"Is that it? Just two"

"Wait let me check," said the mother.

After punching the keys on the laptop, she looked at her daughter. I guess that's it for now. The girl sits down and frowns.

A limousine is going up the road away from the city. It's night time. The window of the limousine opened and inside the Vice President is talking on the phone. After a while, she holds the phone in her hand and smiled. The limousine cruised away from the city.

Miles away a minibus parked outside a house. A man and a woman got out of the van and forced open the door. They went inside and carefully wrapped two bodies before carrying the bodies into the van. Soon after they left. On the way, the van driver phoned someone.

"Job done. Place clear"

The woman who is in the back of the van is checking the corpses of the couple.

"Did you get their IDs?"

"Yes."

The van arrived at a property. After making sure that no one was watching, they carried the two bodies into the property. They closed the doors behind them and left.

A man walked into a pub and ordered lunch and a pint of beer. He waited at the counter. He looked around before getting his eyes fixed on the television mounted on the side.

"Please, can you turn the volume up?" He asked the sales assistant.

The anchor-woman on television is presenting the afternoon bulletin.

"This just in. A couple were found dead in their house this morning. The circumstances of their deaths are still unclear, but police were informed. It is believed that although not yet formally confirmed, the property belonged to Sammy and Nancy Plivdasnki, the former owners of the Breathbank company. After all the allegations and the charges that were expected to be brought against them, it is understood that the circumstances of their deaths are not treated as suspicious. Sources close to the person who found them this morning suggested that they took their own lives. I will have an update later in the afternoon. Mariana reporting for Oceans channel."

The man sat down as the sales assistant lowered the

volume.

"You don't know who to trust anymore nowadays. A young man full of life and his wife expecting a baby taking their own lives? I don't buy it. Do you know that he is the founder of the Breathbank? And who owns it now?"

The man looked a bit upset. The sales assistant looked on for a while without saying anything.

"I understand they were calling for his head?"

"Yes, so that they can dispossess him. What else?"

"I don't have the true facts, but rumor has it that he set up Senator Roy and blackmailed him."

"But does that also not make sense that he tried to help him? He was a bright kid. Even before that he owned a research lab in the city which they set on

fire."

"He might have been a bright person but experimenting on humans? That a no. No matter what. Kidnapping resulting in death, I think he was carrying a big burden on his shoulder," said the sales assistant.

"Earlier sources said that the woman was in police custody, after the death of the Senator they changed and claimed that she was never in police custody. What do we believe? Rumors have it that the big man himself was seen making deals with this young man. Maybe he worked for them?"

The sales assistant remained silent.

Sammy entered a very small basement room and saw Nancy laying on the bed. She quickly sits up straight as he entered the room.

"Darling, you are back how did it go?"

"This is not what I dreamed of, but I guess we have to accept that. I got the passports we must live tonight and start a new life. She said that if we stayed, something bad might happen to us. She said that they spared us only because I am the one who knows about this research and they might need me in the future," said Sammy.

"What if they find someone else? So, there are no guarantees. Are there?" asked Nancy.

"No guarantees babe, but at least we are together. We must start worrying only about our baby. The rest, we will try to leave all behind us?"

"Let me see the passports?" asked Nancy stretching her hand.

Sammy handed over the passports to her.

"Joseph and Joyce? We should have chosen our own names, I think," said Nancy.

"I have thought about it. But I think I have read somewhere about these two. If memory serves me right, I think they were in research and development just like us."

"Sammy if that's the case then I think they were clean. That makes sense. When they need you in the future, it will be easy to go public at times. I think there is nothing to be afraid of. What can they do to an unborn baby? They can't murder us. Can they?"

"I don't know darling I think we are safe for the meantime," said Sammy.

"You still look worried, is there something else?"

Sammy took a long breath before answering his wife.

"There is something you should know too?"

Sammy sits next to his wife and touched her hands.

"What is it darling?"

Sammy kissed her first.

"One of the conditions is that we should all get the

jabs"

"So?"

"Can't you see it. That way it will be easy for them to kill us?"

"Something wrong with the jabs? Why did you say that?"

"That's a good question. Surprisingly I never even tried to check if their jabs were for real. Now it will be hard. I have no facilities, finance or even permission to carry out any research. There must be something they are covering too. We have to try to find a way to leverage this."

"Sammy still that does not explain your fears about the jab."

Sammy looked at the walls for a while before replying to his wife.

"Oh, the jabs. Once we accept the jabs, our life will be in their hands. We will lose our freedom. See, God gave us our freedom by making us each one unique so that no man can manipulate us. But the recent events have opened a loophole if you like. See these jabs alters a unique combination with a genetically engineered one that can be copied and remade. Although it's unthinkable now, in the future it is possible for them to create doubles themselves. What can stop them from creating death partners themselves?"

"I see what you me"

"Especially the fact that it is compulsory. It's the life of everyone into one person's hands. I don't like it. That's just not me."

"Sammy what if we run away, do we have to live as these two forever or what? Think about our baby, we don't want to raise a baby in a world like this?"

"Part of the deal is that we live as Joseph and Joyce. They will give us where to stay. We will have our freedom, but we can change the names they have given us. Right now, per the world we are dead."

Later that night the couple left the basement and went for a walk. In the vicinity, a man is outside, and people are surrounding him. He seemed to be preaching. Wearing scarfs and hooded jumpers. Sammy and Nancy stopped and listened to the man for a while.

As they arrived a woman was leaving. She looked at the couple and spoke as she was leaving.

"Crazy man, mumbling? Who listens to this?" she walked away.

Sammy and Nancy stopped and listened.

"Although not very smartly dressed the man sounded genuine. His face convinced him that he knew what he was talking about. He sounded like an old era preacher. He walked from left to right and sometimes stopped in the middle. He looked face to face with his audience. People kept coming and leaving, some just giving him just a few minutes of their time.

"Say no to the jabs! They are stealing your future, your freedom, your rights. You are putting your life into the hands of one person. This is not an act of

God, this is the work of the devil. You will all perish. God made you unique. There is only one you. The jabs will make all of you the same inside. Envy and jealous shall cause you to kill one another. Wars and fighting shall be your future. They will set one against each other until you are all dead. Refuse the jabs today. Unite and together you shall succeed."

Sammy hugged his wife and walked away from the preacher.

"To some extent he is right. It's like making the Vice President God himself. So many things can go wrong. So many people can be given the same identical jabs. They are not experienced enough to create so many unique jabs to cater for the whole earth. My idea was simple. Save your breath, deposit your own breath and re-breath in the future."

Nancy kept quiet for some time.

"Maybe it's best if we are all identical. I mean, when we all have the same genetic makeup. Maybe that will be easy for doctors and scientists to understand more about humans and how we can live for hundreds of years. I think it is a gray area. There is more we can learn"

"Nancy, are you saying that we should get the jabs?"

"I am just saying that there are a lot of things we just don't know yet."

Somewhere in Russia Andrei and Faye are in the car driving in snowy weather. They have been driving for a while now. Faye is sitting in the passenger seat looking outside the window. She saw forests, trees, mountains and frozen lakes along the way. Andrei looked at her and the road ahead occasionally.

"Worried, huh?"

"You can say that. Are we going to be on the run all the time? It's funny, with my papa we were always in the lab. I am not used to this."

"There is a time for everything. I will teach you how to survive in the real world. We have to find a way to try to stop her."

Faye smiled and looked outside.

"Ha, you found a way already. Just like your father."

"Leave my papa out of this. This is my own decision, not his."

"I know, I mean you would rather die than to kill"

"What makes you say that?"

"I am old, but I am not stupid you know. I was not born yesterday. I saw the formula. Exactly like the one your father gave Aija. Are you suicidal? I thought that all these months you were making your own, unique one. Surely, I can stand in your father's shoes and say that's not the correct way to handle this situation."

Faye looked outside the window without saying anything.

"It's not very hard to make your own. You should have spent those months making your own. Prove her jabs are fake. Create a real one. It's tough, but that's life nothing is easy in life."

"Andrei, either way, she is going to kill us. Look where is my father today. Who are those people chasing us the other day? I can't be on the run all the time. I love researching in the lab all the time. This is not just me."

After a while, Faye started dozing off. Andrei looked at her and smiled. The car drove for some time before Andrei noticed that a car was behind them. They traveled for a stretch of the road and the car seemed to have disappeared behind.

Occasionally, Andrei would keep an eye on the road.

Twenty minutes or so the car appeared in the rearview mirror.

This time it came very close and clipped the back of Andrei and Faye's car. The car swerved and Faye woke up screaming. "What's going on?"

She sat up straight and looked at the back. She saw a car with two men behind them and one of them seemed to be holding a gun.

"Oh no!"

She shouted looking at Andrei and the road ahead.

"Stay down!" shouted Andrei.

The other car advanced and tried to push their car out of the road. Andrei lost control for some time and the car came off the road for a while before finding its way back on the road. A gunshot sound sends Faye covering her ears ducking down. The bullet hits the passenger side-view mirror shattering it into pieces. This time Andrei pushed the other car off-road as it tried to overtake them. The car following them and soon found its way back onto the road and the chase continued.

"Get this, hold the steering wheel for a while," asked Andrei opening the glove compartment of the car. He reached for a gun and checked the bullet magazine. He slummed it back and removed the safety pin. He looked in the road ahead and the other car was coming in front of them. Andrei noticed that their car was partly on the wrong side. Quickly he veered the car sending Faye screaming and the other car pressing the horn constantly.

Faye looked backward wishing that the other car following them have a head-on collision with the oncoming traffic.

She slumped back in her passenger seat looking sad.

"Don't worry. I don't think they want to kill us. She wants us alive?"

"What makes you say that?"

"Instincts, I guess."

Faye relaxed after hearing that she looked back and the car was still following them.

"Just like in the old days. I think they are trying to corner us. We should keep our distance for now."

CHAPTER TEN

Somewhere in the suburbs, the phone rang, and a woman got up and picked the phone up. She answered the call before covering the mouthpiece of the phone and shouted upstairs.

"Constantine it's yours. Come downstairs"

She laid the phone on the table and was about to sit down when the girl shouted something to her from the upstairs.

"Who is it? I will be down in a minute!"

"It's your sister!"

A young lady in her mid-twenties came running downstairs. She picked up the phone."

"Halo, sister, how are you?"

"Can you come over there is something I want to talk to you about?"

Later.

"I knew we should have talked about this, but I went ahead and had the jab. I don't know how this will affect us. I was scared you know."

"We are twins, I think we should have talked about this. Don't you think that can affect us as twins?"

"I know but I was scared you would refuse. I was reading all these stories on the Internet of twins dying at the same time in circumstances unrelated just because they were twins. So, I had this jab. Ever since I feel different. I guess this is messing me up. I don't feel like I used to do toward you. For some reason, this is the first time we have been apart for such a long time. I am scared you know."

"So, what do you want? You are asking me now. Why you didn't ask me the first time before you went to get the jabs?"

"Honestly, I did it for us, for you. We are twins but my lifestyle is totally different from yours. I was afraid that if that was true that twins were dying at the same time somehow, I wanted to avoid that."

"Constantine, what makes you think that now it's safe to get the jabs?"

"Yes, it's safe now you can get your own chromosome compositing different from mine. That way whatever happens to me you will not be affected. I will be at peace knowing that even if I am to die today, you will have a normal life."

A car is parked outside in town. A girl is sitting

inside she is chewing gum. She blows a bubble of chewing gum and a huge ball appeared covering her lips. She pushed air inside the ball, and it burst. She licked the gum back into her mouth. She checked her time.

"Come on what is taking you so long," she said aloud but sitting alone in the car. She looked in front of her but on the other side of the road. She saw another woman walking toward the bank in the city center. She quickly took her bag from the passenger seat. She took out a blonde wig. She stuck her lips together and made a kissing-like sound. She applied lipstick and flicked down the mirror in the car. She looked at herself in the small mirror. She took an empty bag and walked toward the woman.

They met and the two women hugged each other and snogged each other for some time. They kept in each other's arms for some time until the pager of one of the women beeped. The woman from the car followed the other woman very closely. The woman in front arrived at the door. She punched in a code into the machine at the door. A small film-like ribbon protracted on the machine in front of her. She placed the tip of her tongue on the ribbon and the ribbon disappeared after being retracted inside the machine. After a few seconds, the door opened. The woman in front entered the building. The following woman did the same. Punched in some code first and when a ribbon protracted from one side. She placed the tip of her tongue and waited. A flashing message appeared on the screen asking her to try again.

Another ribbon protracted and appeared on the machine. She licked the ribbon again. After a few seconds, the door opened. She walked inside and quickly followed the leading woman who was waiting for her. They entered the corridor one behind the other. On the other end of the corridor, there was an office. A man was there, sitting on his desk typing something on the computer.

"Wait until I have entered the office, then proceed to the room on your left. Enter the code and lick the ribbon, do the same as before."

The first woman touched her cleavage and straightened her blouse-collar and swaggered inside. Straight into the office. The man opened the door by flicking a button from underneath his desk. The woman sat on his desk blocking the view to the corridor. She sat on the desk showing her inner thighs. The man looked at her and stopped what he was doing.

"How come you are always busy? Do you have time to yourself maybe for a glass of wine or something?"

"Lately, not really, this has to be done. It's nearly month-end and they want all these figures, otherwise, I am in deep trouble."

"I just thought that maybe today we should spend some time together to get to know each other, say after work?"

The woman looked at her wristwatch and gently slides her hand down her thigh. The man followed the directional movement of the woman's hand. He sat back resting in the chair comfortably. He breathed hard and looked at the woman.

"Honestly, I have been busy since my colleague left. She is on vacation right now. I have been doing two jobs lately, covering for her."

"So, what time did you say?" asked the woman looking at her wristwatch. After a while, a man heard a noise as if a door was being closed. He looked to see what was going on, but the woman distracted her putting her cleavage in his face. The woman looked at her watch again and a beep sound came out of the pager. She looked at the page.

"Okay, if you are busy, I guess I have to get stuck with my job as well. She walked out of the man's office and entered the other office."

"Oh, my God! Why is the safe open? Why is everything on the floor? Who was in here? I just arrived at what is going on here?"

The man rushed to the other office with the safe. The safe has been emptied. All the samples were gone, and the cash too had gone.

The man quickly got on the phone and phoned the Head Office.

"Hello! All the samples are gone and the cash too."

"When did this happen? Were the samples there at the start of work?"

"I don't know I didn't check; I know I am supposed to, but it has been busy lately for me. I just entered the office and went straight to my office. The other staff members are still on vacation. It is me and the other manager only."

"So, when did you last checked the samples? When is the last time you been in that office?"

"Let's see, I have been there for eh, three days now. I was alone in the office and I was very busy. I normally check every day but this week, to be honest, I am doing work for two people. I just couldn't find the time."

"Is it possible that it could be the other manager who did it?"

"Highly unlikely. She was not here either since last week. She just got back today I swear I saw her walk in through the door. She did not enter that room."

"So, who did it?" asked the operator from the Head Office.

"Honestly I don't know the samples could have been taken over the weekend."

"In that case, there is not much we can do. I will see if I can send someone later to look at this"

The man walked up and down and then sat down.

The other female manager entered his office.

"When did this happen? So, what did the Head Office say."

"I don't know when that happened. There is not much they can do. The place is new, just to think we opened the place a few weeks ago, not even any cameras are functioning."

"Whose samples, were they?"

"Honestly like I said I had no time to check. I just received the samples just last week, and I signed for the samples and placed them in the safe. They left me on my own to do work for four people. Thank you, you are back at least you will help. They opened a new branch when we are understaffed. I can't believe it?"

"Where are the receipts? I will try to find out whose samples, were they?"

"Check in the cabinet."

The woman opened the cabinet and took out a file and looked at the receipts.

She looked at the man with wide-open eyes and an open mouth.

"The samples belonged to the President!"

"Oh, my God! I am dead?"

The Vice President is sitting in her office. She heard a knock at the door.

"Come in."

The usher opened the door.

"Mrs. Vice President, the chief security officer is here to see you."

"Show him in."

A man dressed in a uniform entered the office holding his hat in his hand. He was very swift and walked into fashion. He looked straight up raising his chin up. He arrived at the desk and stood in front of the chair.

"Sit. What brings you here?"

"We have a problem."

"I am listening"

"There was a burglary. We can't figure out how that happened. But…."

"But what?" asked the Vice President.

"The samples are gone. The President's samples are gone. I assure you I will personally do whatever it takes to make sure that no risk will befall the President."

Angrily the Vice President rose from her seat, her face red shaking with anger.

"What? Who did that? Who on earth would steal the President's samples?" She walked up and down the room.

"Why would one still the presidents' samples? Find the samples. If they get into the wrong hands, we are doomed. Damn! These people should fear me. Who is behind this? Find out who is behind this?"

The chief security officer left the office leaving the

Vice President traumatized. She walked toward the window and thought for a while. She quickly walked to the desk and picked up the phone.

"It is time to come to my office today without failure." she quickly placed the phone down without even waiting for the other person to reply.

Later that afternoon Sammy (now called Joseph) is in the Vice President's office. He looked at the pictures on the walls, all the memorabilia and decorations. He got up and walked to the cabinet with achievement awards. Suddenly, the big doors opened, and the Vice President walked in followed by the President. The two are talking together and the atmosphere felt very serious as if something big has happened. They both sat around the table.

The Vice President advised Joseph to sit.

"The reason we called you Mr. Joseph, is that we need your help to try to recover some samples stolen yesterday from one of our offices."

"Whose samples if I may ask?"

The Vice President and the President cast each other a quick glance before the President nodded his head. The Vice President leaned forward.

"This should not leave this room. The samples belonged to the President."

"President? What's in for me?"

"Mr. Joseph, you are eternally indebted to the President and now he is presenting to you a chance to get even with him. Find out who did this. No harm shall befall the President. You understand me?"

"I can only ask for one favor. If I help you recover these samples will we go wherever we want and choose our own names after this? And never to wait for you to call us back?"

The Vice President looked at the President.

"OK, this will be your last assignment."

"OK, thank you, Mr. President, and thank you, Mrs. Vice President. If you can show me out, I will get started."

A large door opened, and three men and a woman are in the laboratory.

"Ladies and gentlemen, I present to you professor Joseph please work with him. He will recover the stolen samples."

The days that followed Joseph was relentless in the lab designing formulas to try to solve the puzzle.

He called in a programmer and logged software onto his handheld device. He uploaded some samples on the devices and tried it. After the results, he knew that he was ready. He was given the address. One evening he got hired Ferrari and traveled to the bank in the city. He parked outside and firstly observed the people going in and out of the bank.

He checked how many people entered the bank at a given time. He took pictures of each one.

He walked toward the bank. He arrived at the entrance and observed the entry system. He waited at the machine and used the device he brought to downloaded information of all the people who had logged into the device for the past two weeks. He rang the bell. A man opened the door and walked back inside inviting Joseph.

They entered an office. Joseph introduced himself and first requested to check the room where the samples were taken.

"So, in your view, who do you think did this?" asked Joseph.

"I really had no clues it's hard to tell"

"I need access to the list of all the people who logged on that day and the previous week."

After meeting with the bank manager Joseph was introduced to the female bank manager who found out that the samples were missing.

Later that night Joseph was in the lab analyzing the samples. He looked at everyone who had entered the bank for the last week before the discovery. He made a profile of all the people.

Professor Zunis came in and looked at him.

"Any luck with profiling yet?"

"No luck, no one fits, everyone who entered the building has been accounted for. All the samples and the log list checked out. I collected separate chromosome makeups using my device which I created and matched the list from my device and the list from the bank. Everyone is accounted for. I have checked and eliminated all those who work there. I then checked all the visitors and customers everyone is accounted for. I was expecting to pick up some chromosome composition not registered by the bank's device but registered on my device but no one at all."

"Could it be an inside job?"

"I can't say for sure but highly unlikely."

The following days Joseph spends his time in the lab and when the weekend arrived, he carried his possessions home.

Nancy (now called Joyce) was home, pregnant and eagerly waiting for the return of her husband.

"I can't figure out how one can pass through all security checks without being detected and steal the President's chromosome samples."

"Can I see? I might help you figure out what happened," said Joyce.

Joseph gave his wife everything to have a look at while he went to take a shower.

Joyce went over and over the reports, but she could not figure out what had happened.

After taking the shower Joseph brought a glass of wine and sat next to his wife. He poured his wine. His wife refused the wine mentioning pregnancy as an excuse. She had had her daily allowance already.

Joseph kissed her belly and rubbed it talking to an unborn baby.

Joyce was looking over the files trying to link everything.

Joseph sat up straight and took over from his wife. He sipped his wine and kissed Joyce.

"Your tongue taste wine are you trying to get my baby drunk?" asked Joyce rubbing her tummy.

"That's it."

He got up and quickly entered the spare room. He brought back a copy of the device used as part of the security system. He connected it to the mains and switched it on.

He asked his wife to lick the ribbon protracted and download the information.

Perfect match to the chromosome makeup the saliva was matched to his wife. He tried himself. He licked the ribbon and downloaded the results. Another perfect match, the saliva sample was his. He goes into the bathroom and brushed his mouth without and toothpaste to remove the wine.

He came back and snogged his wife and deliberately drew some of her saliva. He then licked the ribbon and downloaded the results. The results were inconclusive.

"I thought I got the answers but still, no answers."

The couple put everything away and bonded as if there is no tomorrow.

The whole weekend Joseph, whenever he had free time, kept trying he looked at this case.

Come Sunday night the two are in the bedroom.

"I am afraid I have to go back to work. I will come back midweek to check up on you, but I will phone you every day."

"Darling I have been thinking about our baby lately. What name should we give her?"

"Honestly I haven't thought about it. But I would like to name her after you."

"Oh, that's sweet of you?"

Joseph got up and entered the bathroom and started brushing his teeth.

"Darling what if they are twins?"

"What?"

"What if the babies are twins what names we can give them if they are a boy and a girl?"

"I never thought of it that way. What if they are twins?"

Joseph without finishing brushing his teeth quickly looked at his files and checked if anyone had a twin but no one had a twin.

Monday morning, everyone is at the briefing in the Vice President's office.

"Morning everyone. I am a bit disappointed that after a week we still can't figure out what happened and who is responsible. We have the brightest heads in the country, and you are telling me that you can't find who is behind this? Mr. Joseph, I want you to go back there and don't leave any stone unturned."

Joseph later that morning headed back to the bank. He was in the car trying to figure out what happened that day. On his way, he saw twins going into the shopping mall. He found somewhere safe to park. He got his device and approached the twins.

"Excuse me, I work for the President. I am doing an experiment. I am researching twin behavior and I don't know if you can help me? I assure you that the samples I get will not be stored but destroyed straight away after the experiment. This will take a few minutes. I can buy you lunch if you like after."

The twins agreed and Joseph took the samples and downloaded the reports. Even though the chromosomes were similar they were identified as different by the system.

"So even twins cannot use the saliva sample to open the door. So, what really happened that day," asked Joseph speaking to himself.

The male bank manager was in and others had come back from the vacations. Joseph interviewed the bank manager again, but still, he left with nothing.

Later that day professor Zunis and Joseph are having lunch.

"I have never felt so hopeless like this before."

"There is something we are missing"

"I think If I were you, now it's time to start eliminating them one by one. A deep analysis of everyone present that day. Start with the employees then the customers."

CHAPTER ELEVEN

The Vice President entered the lab and found Joseph's laptop. She checked the information and found out that he was running a database search she flipped through his files and looked at the reports. She checked his findings and possible explanations. She looked at all the employees and saw the male managers file. He had a girlfriend, they worked together but at the time of the break-in, she was not at work. She was on vacation. The other manager had no relationship information on the file. She checked the files of every other employee and found out that it was only her without any relationship information. She made copies of her file and left the lab.

Later that day the Vice President is in her office. She is sitting on her desk. She picked up the phone and rang a number.

"Yes. Can you run a background check on someone I am sending the files right now?"

There was a knock on the door.

"Come in"

Joseph entered the office and sits down.

"You called for me?"

"Yes, Mr. Joseph. I would like to take this opportunity to thank you for all your work at such short notice. Can you leave your report on my desk? I will take over from here. I will assign the task to someone else. You are dismissed and have a wonderful life."

"Yes, but I haven't finished yet I run a background check of all the employees"

"Yes. Don't worry it's okay. Go home, your wife needs you."

Joseph remained seated for a while before getting up and leaving. He brought the file before saying goodbyes.

The phone rang in the Vice President's office.

"Hello, Vice President speaking."

"Yes, Mrs. Vice President. I just sent you a file through your fax machine. I think you might want to look at this."

"Hold the line," said the Vice President.

She stood up and walked to the fax machine. She picked up the papers and looked at the picture and notes just faxed.

"Yes. What can you tell me about this person?"

"At first, I thought sisters, but I think I can say, lovers, secret lovers to be precise."

"You have an address?"

"It's not the address you want it's the chromosome makeup that will shock you. Check the next fax."

"Just a moment."

The fax machine beeped and started printing the copies.

"Yes, let's see."

There was a moment of silence.

"Are you sure that's not for the same person? How can two different people have the same chromosome makeup? I thought this was prohibited and against the law."

"I thought so too, but I have found out that in their circles it's permitted, till death do us apart?"

"I see, I always overlooked these."

"So, till death do us apart. Wherever you go, I go yeah?"

"Exactly! Mrs. Vice President."

"Thank you very much I will be in touch if I need your services."

"Pleasure is mine, Mrs. Vice President."

A limousine strolled down the road and parked outside the bank on the other side of the road. The back window slowly open. A woman with sunglasses and a soft floppy wide woolen hat looked outside before slowly closing the window. A van stopped outside, and the passenger got out and walked at the back of the van. He opened the back door and took out a bunch of lovely red lovers and an envelope. He walked to the glass doors of the bank and rang the bell. A woman opened the door after a few minutes.

"Can you sign here?" asked the man.

The woman quickly took the flowers and the envelope inside. She knocked on the female manager's office door and left the flowers and the envelope on her desk. A woman walked on the pavement outside in high heels. She looked at the parked limo and the window of the limo opened. A woman in the limo waved her hand and soon closed the window. The woman on the pavement smiled and proceeded to go into the bank.

"There is a parcel for you which I left on your desk."

"OK, thank you," smiled Sylvia.

Sylvia quickly opened the note on the flowers and then took the envelope and opened it. She looked outside and took her bag. She placed the envelope in her bag and walked out of the bank and toward the limousine. She entered the limousine.

"Who are you? What do you want?"

"I have a business proposal for you. Tell me who you gave the samples to, take the money and walk away."

The woman tried to get out of the limo, but the doors of the limousine suddenly lock up.

"I don't know what you are talking about."

"Trust me you don't want to mess up with me you know. Do it for her. You will be together forever. I just want my samples back."

The woman looked scared and looked at the lady who she was talking to.

"OK let me convince you first."

The lady in the limo clicked her fingers together,

and the limousine started moving.

"No. I can't go with you. I am at work, drop me here," said Sylvia, the woman who works in the bank.

"Don't worry about that, I gave you an alibi. A car parked outside the bank and a woman inside waited eagerly to kiss her lover and seal the deal. Woman meets woman the two, exchanged saliva making sure it's 100% match. Woman opened the door gave saliva samples and entered the building. The second woman waited for a certain interval to make it look like the first woman has forgotten something maybe in the car or something like that. The first woman goes to the office and distracts the male manager who seems not to cope with work. The second woman entered the bank, using lovers, the same genetic makeup system thinking that its first woman then granted access the second time around. The second woman entered the safe office, presumably looking for money. Money in the safe gone but still not enough. The second woman grabbed everything thinking maybe of value and left. Second woman, I presume dressed like first woman same hair or, a wig and wearing the same clothes. The first woman pretends to flirt with the male but in fact-checking time. The first woman receives a text message job done, she gets up and after teasing the male manager goes into the office with the safe for the first time since last week. The male manager is the witness. The first woman panicked and screamed.

The male manager came running. Job done. So, you tell me how did I do?" asked the women in the limousine.

"I still don't know what you are talking about," replied the woman.

Angrily the woman in the limo puts her hands around Sylvia's neck.

"Don't lie to me. Who sent you? Why the samples? What did you do with the samples? I warn you don't lie to me."

The woman in the limousine takes off the woolen floppy hat and glasses.

"Mrs. Vice President!"

Shouted Sylvia shocked and afraid.

"That's right, it's me are you going to cooperate or what?"

Outside a school, a woman is standing there and has been there for a good twenty minutes. She walked up and down. She is wearing black jeans, and a pink hooded top. She rubbed her hands together and blew hot air in there. When a car approached her, she would stop and wait to see if the car would stop for her or not. As soon as the car has passed-by, she would continue pacing again up and down. A dark hammers car came from the other side. A man was driving the car and playing loud rock music. He opened the window and indicated to stop but did not stop. He passed the lady, and the lady started running after the car. The driver stopped the car and quickly reversed the car nearly knocking down the woman.

"Watch it asshole! What do you think you are doing? You nearly killed me."

"How can I help you?"

"Can you take me somewhere up the road I need to get some cash? I am scared to go on my own."

"Are you selling something or what?"

"You can say that. You want to see?"

"Is it illegal or what? What is it? Let me see?"

The woman handed over the aluminum flask, but the driver looked at it and threw it outside. The flask landing on the grass nearby.

"What is this? I thought you have good stuff. Get out of my car."

"Are you crazy? What the hell are you doing? That is worth millions. You are a crazy fool."

The car drove away before coming to a screeching halt and reversed instantly. The woman on seeing the car reversing picked up the flask and started running away.

He got out and followed the woman.

"Listen if it's worth millions I will go with you!" Shouted the man.

The woman kept running.

"Cross my heart, I will take you there, but I will need a cut!"

The woman stopped and started walking back.

The man turned around and started walking toward the car he did not stop for her. He jumped in and waited. The woman jumped in too and the car drove off playing loud music.

"So, are you going to tell me what it is?"

The woman hesitantly showed the flask to the man. Look what it written, underneath.

"Don't worry I won't throw it outside again, let go."

The man grabbed the flask and read at the bottom without looking where the car was going."

A lorry sounded the horn and flashed its headlights.

"Watch it, are you trying to get us killed?"

"Nick David, President of the United States of America. Samples."

Quickly, the driver suddenly applied the brakes, and the car leaned forward sending the flask flying and leaving the lady hanging on the roof rails.

"That's illegal that's US property. I can't get involved. I don't want to get into trouble. How much were you going to sell it for?"

"I heard my mum say it's worth $200 000 but the man up there said he can give me $50 000.

"Your mum?"

The man looked shocked and saddened.

"I thought you were going to say your lover?"

"Do you know my mum? What makes you say that? People always think that we are dikes. She is my mum."

"I just guessed based on the fact that you are too emotional. I just thought that you are… eh, you know"

The lady laughed.

"So how much are you going to give me?"

"If she is your mum, then I can give you $100 000."

The men opened the glove compartment and took an envelope and gave it to the lady.

"Deal! Flask is yours."

"Do you want a lift back or you will be okay?"

"I will be okay, more than enough thanks?"

The hammer car sped off leaving the lady in the road and when the lady was off sight, the car stopped, and the driver rang someone.

"Abort. I repeat Abort. I got the samples. Mum and daughter. I repeat. Abort."

The driver hits the steering wheel with both hands and cursed. After a while, he received a phone call. He turned back the car and started going back.

"$200 000 in that envelope take it and go I want the samples back intact? What were you thinking? It's the President's samples. I could have shot you dead. I have nothing against dikes, but you are crazy. Who on earth would have the same chromosome make up as your lover?"

The woman looked away before she replied.

"My daughter."

The Vice President looked shocked.

"Stop the limo right now!" shouted the Vice President.

She picked up the phone and called someone.

"Abort the mission. I repeat. Mother and daughter. Abort!"

"What is going on? Is my daughter safe?"

"You think you can steal the President's sample and get away with it?"

"The samples were just a decoy. We were after the money only. We only realized after. I swear, take me and leave my daughter. Take back your money."

The Vice President picked up the phone and dialed a number and listened.

The door of the limo opened, Sylvia got out quickly and thanked the Vice President. The limousine sped off leaving Sylvia with a bag with the money inside. The Vice President checked her watch and rang someone.

"Resume the mission."

Sylvia walked a few steps and opened the bag. She looked inside to find the money and a flask. Surprised about the flask. She took out the flask and looked at the bottom; Nick David the President of the United States of America; Samples."

"No! My daughter!" she collapsed and died.

The driver of the hammer car jumped out of the car and walked forward. He stopped and picked up an envelope he flicks the bunch of clean banknotes and looked at the dead lady. He jumped in the car and drove off.

A chilly night over the city. A cat jumped from the nearby bin and meows walking down the road. It stopped and sniffed at something in the road before walking across the road. It reached the bins outside one of the houses across the road. The cat jumped on top of the full bin and sniffed the rubbish searching for food. The cat found something and jumped down with it and started eating it. A car comes from down the road and as it passes through. The headlights shined at the cat. The cat stopped eating and picked up what looked like part of a human face, a nose like thing is seen. The car turned around a bend and disappeared. The cat walked toward the house.

The basement light of the house is on. Suddenly a loud scream came from the basement. Inside the basement, an old man with a young man who is strapped on the bed. The man is holding a knife in one hand and what looked like a human nose in the other. The man on the bed screamed in agony. The man threw the flesh in a tray on the table next to him. He returned to the young man sleeping on the bed. He kneeled and cuts another nose like flesh from the man's chest.

The young man screamed in agony.

"There you go, good boy, was that bad?"

He breathed heavily. He walked to the sink basin and washed his hands. He grabbed the towel and cleaned his hands and dosed his face before coming back to the bed. A young woman entered the room with a basin and a liquid inside. She opened the sterilizing tub with cotton wool. She starts cleaning the man on the bed removing all the blood.

"Did you tell the jab company about all this?" asked the woman sounding very sad.

"We told them. It's the same story every time. He just had another jab, but the condition has improved a little. Some genetic mutations. I don't know what to do. I have tried everything."

"What did the hospital say?"

"Same story can't be reversed but to keep cutting the noses from his chest each time they grow."

"It must be stressful and traumatizing."

"I have never seen anything like this. It was worse the first time. I just couldn't stand how my son grew two more noses. These jabs are not safe."

"Maybe ask them to give him a different jab?"

"Don't you think that I tried. They said we must wait for a year that was nine months ago. Ever since I was just cutting off these whenever they grow.

It's traumatizing."

"I have a friend who knows someone who can help."

"Maybe we should invite him one day, see what he says"

A car drove along a busy road in the city. People are blocking the road ahead as they are marching in the city. Car drivers ahead are blasting their horns, but the crowd remained in the road marching forward. They are holding posters and placards. Behind a car slows down to match the speed of the other cars ahead. The driver uses the screen wipes to clean the window. A woman is sitting at the back of the car.

"What is going on?"

"These protesters every day hitting the streets."

"What seems to be the problem."

"Who knows?"

The woman looked outside at the protesters. Some are holding banners that said that the jabs are not safe. Some protesters are walking next to her car. The woman opened the window, and a man leans down to talk to the woman.

"The jabs are not safe. A lot of genetic defects. No one knows why and to make things worse no one listens. We want answers?"

In an office, somewhere in the city, a woman is standing at the window. She looked outside. There are a lot of people outside holding banners and posters.

"This is getting out of hand now. What seems to be the problem?"

The professor breathed heavily before he sits up straight.

"There was always to be problems like this. Some people are reacting badly to the jabs. It's understandable. The problem is that we can't administer another jab before the first one wears off. We have to wait at least for a year."

"So, for all these people there is nothing you can do?"

"Correct Mrs. Vice President."

"Is there a way you can clean all this mess? Honestly. It's a one egg spoils the rest situation. I can't tolerate that. Out of the billions, we jeopardize everything because of a handful of cases. No. We have achieved a lot. See what you can do about this."

"Are you sure?"

"Of course, I am sure. I don't want people standing outside my office every day like that. Come and see. Eh, look. That's not a good image at all. Do whatever it takes."

The professor got up and walked to the window. He stood there for some minutes.

"OK. I will see what I can do."

He walked outside and approached the crowd.

"We are very sorry that some of you haven't been so lucky. We understand that. All we are asking from you is that we need time to try to find a way to resolve this. In the meantime, there is nothing we can do. We have to wait for the first wave to wear off before we can start thinking of doing anything else."

"We are not going anywhere until we have seen the Vice President herself."

"I am afraid that she is very busy now, but I promise she will address you soon."

A woman dragged her son from behind her and holds him in her arms.

"Tell that to my son"

Everyone looks at her. The professor looked at the kid and closed his eyes for a while. The son had another eye growing between the upper lip and the nose.

"Listen, everyone! Can you all go to where you were given the jabs as soon as possible."

The professor walked back into the office.

"So?" asked the Vice President.

"They refused to go until you have addressed them."

"You know I can't do that. I can't be associated with failure."

"Mrs. Vice President, what do you suggest we do."

"How bad is it?" asked the Vice President.

"Very bad and on a scale, out of 10, 10 being the worst. I would say 11."

"Damn!"

There was a moment of silence.

"Pair them."

"Excuse me? Mrs. Vice President"

"You heard me. Pair them."

Three months later a father whose son had genetic defects growing noses on each chest is in the hospital foyer talking to the doctors.

"How did it go is my son going to be okay?"

The doctor looked at him without saying anything. He placed his hand on his shoulder.

"I am sorry he didn't make it"

The father sat down, shocked, he didn't think that

was that serious. He cried inconsolably.

pg. 262

CHAPTER TWELVE

Somewhere in a village in Russia Faye and Andrei are working in a homemade lab. The past months they have worked together tirelessly.

"I think we should go back to the city. The past six months we have been in hiding I think they might have given up now. I really miss city life," said Faye sitting down.

Andrei smiled and looked at her.

"Honestly, this was my dream. Come to the countryside and enjoy life."

He looked at Faye and all the surroundings.

"So?"

"I don't know to be honest. I think on my own it's depressing. Honestly together I loved it. I think I have a lot of thinking to do."

"I think I had a good time. I remembered my papa. That was me and him, for most of the time."

"Only regret. Country life makes me feel very old."

"So, city life, huh?"

"I guess city life it is."

Andrei is driving heading to the city. He is unrecognizable. Faye looked at him and laughs.

"You look different with all that beard."

"Hope we will be safe in the city. I am concerned about you. I think you should find someone who loves you and go on vacation. I think you deserve time away from all this."

"Andrei, I was starting to think that. I am not a little girl anymore. Papa would have been happy to see me like this."

"Where ever he is, I know, he is proud of you."

The two exchanged quick glances before Andrei concentrated on driving.

After a few hours of driving. Driving fatigue kicking in as Andrei veered off the road before finding his way back on the road.

"Do you want me to drive?" asked Faye.

"I am OK. Just lost it a bit, but I will be okay." Half an hour later, a car came up behind them.

"Fasten your seat belt stay down. I think we have company."

The driver of the car at the back made his intentions clear. He wanted them out of the road. He edged forward and clipped the back of their car. The car swerved off the road for a while before it got back on the road. The passenger in the car at the back took out a gun and placed half of his body outside through the window and aimed for the tires of the car. Andrei swerved from side to side. Soon the other car was side by side with theirs. An oncoming car blasted the horn continuously and just before the cars were close together the other car dropped the speed and quickly moved to the left, giving way to oncoming traffic.

"Why can't you use the gun? You just sit there I thought you have grown up. Still, want to die Shot back?"

"Me? Ha? Are you sure? OK" said Faye.

"When someone is trying to kill you. What do you do?"

Faye opened the glove compartment and took the gun out. She checked the bullet magazine and opened the window. She came out of the window half her body hanging outside the window and aimed. She squeezed the trigger and fired a shot. The car at the back swerved before the passenger of the car at the back opened fire too. He fired bullets aggressively.

Faye ducked, and the chase continued. The other car edged forward and came side by side. Andrei steered very hard toward the car pushing it out of the road. The car drove back and bangs the side of Andrei's car, sending it out of the road. Shots were fired and Andrei found his way back on the road. Faye looked at Andrei, he seemed concentrated on driving. Faye knocked parts of the broken side window off with the handle of the gun. She placed her hand out and shoots.

In the car at the back, the driver drove for a while and then looked at his passenger. The passenger slumped to the side of the door.

"Yanka! Yanka"

The driver shouted juggling between driving and checking his friend. His friend was dead he had been shot in the head and only now has the driver noticed, blood is dripping down his right side. Ahead there was a broken-down car. Andrei maneuvered his car avoiding the broken-down car on the roadside which was partly protruding onto the road. Yugosnki juggling between checking Yanka and driving. I only noticed the parked car last minute. He swerved to avoid the car on the roadside at the same time coming in front of oncoming traffic. He panicked and quickly goes back to his driving roadside at the last minute to avoid a head-on collision, but he lost control after that sending the car spinning before bursting into flames.

Faye took her head out of the car through the window and looked at the back. The car that was following them was in flames. She smiled and placed back her head in the car. She looked at Andrei, but Andrei did not look at her. The car started swerving on the road. Faye noticed that something was wrong. She grabbed the steering wheel and checked on Andrei who slumped to the left. She touched him and felt blood on his back. He had been shot on his back. The car veered off the road before Faye frantically fought to control the car. She pulled up the hand brake sending the car spinning. She was injured and dragged Andrei out of the car.

"You are going to be alright." Said Faye trying to stop the bleeding.

Andrei opened his eyes and looked at Faye. He looked at her for a while. He smiled.

"I am proud of you. Your father and mother are very proud of you."

"Don't talk save energy Andrei," said Faye.

"Just hold on I am going to look for something in the car to stop the bleeding."

Faye got up and looked for a cloth to stop the bleeding.

A gunshot rocketed the woods send her panicking and ducking for cover. She quickly crawled out of the car.

"Oh! No, Andrei! No! Why! No!"

She kneeled and hold Andrei in her arms resting on her laps.

She cries uncontrollably.

Andrei's body is bleeding. A gun is next to his head and his right hand is partly holding the gun and a lot of blood is coming from the back of his head spilling onto Faye's laps.

In the United States of America, a man opened the door. A man wearing shades and a hood over his head entered a building and then a room. There is an operating table on the other side. A table with medical instruments. There is a drip stand next to the bed. There are hospital machines. A young nurse entered the room and walked to the other side and closed the big curtain. She walked back and gave the man a hospital gown and pointed to a room. The man got up and walked to the other room. Minutes later the man returned in a gown. Another man who looked like the doctor entered the room. The man stood in front of the two women and a female nurse. The pair looked at each other. The man in the gown felt embarrassed for a while. "Let's get to business, shall we?"

The man in a gown walked to the bed and laid down. The man who happens to be the operating doctor, and the nurse followed him.

"Do you like any music?" asked the female nurse.

"I would like to see?" said the man pointing at the wall.

"That's fine."

The woman walked toward the wall and clapped her hands.

"Stay still. Don't move."

The nurse returned, and both looked at each other. The man in the gown looked unconcerned. The operation began.

"Volume please?" asked the man halfway through.

The female nurse walked toward the wall and spoke. The volume increased. The woman walked back to the operating table.

The doctor squinted as he removed an ear from the belly button and threw it in the try on the table. The nurse looked at the human ear in the table and twisted her mouth while her eyes were wide open. The man got up and sat down looking at the television.

"Don't move. Mr. President, we haven't finished yet." The man in the gown did not listen to them, instead, he insisted that she increases the volume. He sat down with blood flowing down from his belly button down his groin. The woman looked at the television and walked to increase the volume. She returned, and all three looked at the television and listened to the emergency bulletin.

"It is confirmed that the Vice President died today in her office. The President hasn't been informed yet sources close to him say he is still out of the country on a business trip. No one knows how she died but all the details will be announced once the President has been formally informed."

The President looked in the try to jump from the operating bed in shock and fear at the sight of his extra ear in the try. The ear had been growing on his belly button. The nurse and the doctor locked their eyes together before looking at the President. He stood up, and they stood still and saluted as he walked out.

The people blocked the road heading to the Vice President's office marching to the city. An aerial view shows a huge crowd walking toward the city.

Nicolai is driving his car on his way to the robbed bank in the city. The night before he had received a call from his boss telling him about the bank robbery and the death of the female bank manager. He arrived outside the bank only to find a group of people outside the bank. He got out of the car and walked toward the people standing outside the bank.

"Does the gathering have anything to do with the death of the female manager who died a few days ago?" asked Nikolai.

One of the bank workers was outside his name was Dimitri.

"Sad news, for some reason the manager killed himself. He is still inside. We have called the ambulance, but they said we have to wait for the coroner's van since he is already dead?"

"Excuse me, are you talking about the female manager?" asked Nikolai.

"No. The male manager. Half an hour ago, he shot himself. Blood is all over the walls. He is sitting on his desk dead. The female manager died a few days ago."

"That's a shame. Does this have anything to do with the stolen money or the missing samples?" Asked Nikolai.

"Honestly no one knows. Rumor has it that the samples were recovered as they were stolen by the female manager. Some money was recovered too but I don't know how the manager was involved."

"So, the samples were recovered? Is it true that they belonged to the President?"

"Not sure that was classified information, but I heard something like that."

Nikolai went to speak with the security guard at the door.

"My name is Nikolai I am a reporter. Can I have a quick look inside?"

"No! Authorized personnel only." Replied the security guard at the door.

Nikolai searched his pockets and took out a $50 note and squashed the money inside the security guard's pocket.

"I won't be long I promise less than 5 minutes."

The security guard looked at him first.

"Show me your ID," asked the security guard.

Nikolai flashed his badge and entered.

Through the glass windows, he looked for the weapon but could not find one.

"Was anyone in his office? I can't seem to find the gun?"

"That's not my business you said five minutes," said the security guard.

Nikolai left, he entered his car and looked around for a while.

"So, I would assume that this is just suicide. He locked himself inside and shot himself. Maybe he is involved in the robbery. I was if it could be one of the so-called death partners. But the evidence doesn't support that."

Nikolai placed the recorder down and started the car heading to the Vice President's office.

After all the security checks at the gate. Nikolai went into the lifts. The lift door was about to close before a woman's hand stopped its closing. The woman entered the lift and briefly looked at Nikolai. The woman was gorgeous but in disguise. She had sunglasses and a woolen floppy hat, and a lovely long dress. She had lovely skin. She looked younger than her actual age. If it wasn't for her voice and the way she spoke Nikolai could have thought that she was in her mid-thirties. The voice had some authority connotations that made Nikolai think that she was in her early forties or somewhere there. She spoke with authority sounding ordering and commanding. Nikolai looked at her figure. She was lovely, blessed in every department. Nikolai had never met the Vice President before in person. He was excited to meet her in a few minute's time. He looked at the lifts' lights showing which floor he was in.

The woman all this time she was on the phone. Nikolai could hear the other person who she was talking with. He was not interested in what they were talking about. He remembered going for a long time two weeks now to be precise without man's best companion. The woman looked on top of the lift showing which floor they were going next.

"OK, make sure that everything is in place before I arrive. Bye for now."

Nikolai listened to the last conversation, and he heard the person on the other end talking to the woman say; Ok goodbye Mrs. Vice President has a safe journey.

The lift door suddenly opened the woman rushed out.

"Excuse me, sorry to hear your conversation. Are you the Vice President by any chance?" asked

Nikolai.

The woman stopped and looked at him and shook her head before she disappeared. The lift door closed, and the lift went up to the Vice President's office.

The lift door opened, and the presidential Officer was standing outside the lift. He was standing attentively with his hands behind his back.

"I am afraid you have to live the building Sir. Get back in the lift and make your way out of the building," said the security guard.

"I am Nikolai I am here to see the Vice President."

"Sir. Did you hear what I said? I said make your way downstairs and out of the building."

"But I am here to see the Vice President."

"The Vice President passed away today. Please leave the building now."

"Passed away are you sure? I thought…. Can I see her body?"

"Leave the building Sir. Can't do that Sir."

The lift door opened, and Nikolai entered the lifts. Never confused like this before, he left the building.

The first thing that came to his mind was that it was a death partner linked death. Did it have anything to do with the manager who shot himself, he wondered?

He entered his car and drove to the hospital.

He arrived at the hospital and went to the coroner's office.

Curious he researched the Vice President's attempted assassination. He found out that the person who was killed that day was Viktovha later identified by his dental records.

While at the hospital he investigated the death of Senator Roy. He requested a copy of the autopsy. The coroner was Denise of Russian origin. When he realized that Nicolai was Russian, they spoke in Russian for a long time. The coroner after receiving a bribe admitted that something was wrong with the autopsy report. Whoever completed the autopsy report seemed to have not been professionally trained.

Curious about all this he went to the place where the Senator was buried.

Alexandra was the undertaker at the cemetery. All the official government personnel were buried here. These were not like real graves where people were dug into the ground. Here all the people who were brought here were rich or government officials. The graves could be accessed with authorization. After gaining some hundred dollars, Alexandar conceded and led Nikolai into the chamber of the dead. He had keys to the tomb of the Senator. Curios Nikolai ordered Alexandar to open the tomb. He struggled to find the key at first. At last, he found the key and opened the tomb of Senator Roy. He pulled out the coffin and after a while of looking for the key to the coffin he opened the coffin.

"Where is he!" shouted Nikolai.

"Ha! He should be here instead of the coffin but only these slabs inside."

Nikolai did not wait. Soon after he left and went to his hotel. The next day he left the USA going back to Russia.

The discovery that the Senator was not in his tomb and the fact that he overheard the man speaking to the woman in the lift saying goodbye Vice President. He somehow realized that this was bigger than meets the eye.

Nikolai after arriving in Russia he looked for information about this Viktovha. This took him to a house in the countryside that was registered under the Russian name of the Vice President.

On arrival, he noticed that the house looked empty. It seemed that no one was there for a while.

He broke into the house. There were pictures in one of the drawers. He took them and started looking at them. He saw Viktovha and the Vice President the days she was staying in Russia before she moved to the USA. There was another man in the picture. It was a triangle it seems. The Vice President was standing on a boat with Viktovha and another person referred to as Gezzy. On his laptop, he tried to find out this Gezzy but there was no information referring to any Gezzy. This might have been a code name he thought to himself.

He found another photo with Viktovha and the Vice President. So far what he can say is that they were lovers maybe real partners.

That was the only explanation that made sense.

He found Viktovha's old address on a letter.

He drove his car to the city.

He met Lizzy one of Viktovha's short term girlfriends.

Over a coffee, they talked about Viktovha.

"Just curious. Did Viktovha ever talked about a one Aija to you?"

"I think Andrei at one point. I heard him talk about her."

"Whose is this Andrei?"

"Gezzy was Viktovha's best friend. As far as I know, these two had one girlfriend or something like that."

"Ah, that's Gezzy in the photo?"

"Is this Gezzy still alive and do you know where I can find him?"

"I saw him a few months ago, he is now a shadow of himself. No one bothers about him anymore. At one point, he was the most wanted man in Russia. Now all that is gone. Surely, you can find him at his home. I know his address."

The following day Nikolai went to Andrei's house.

No one was home the places looked deserted. He broke in and entered the house. He looked everywhere for clues. It started making sense while he was inside. The two Viktovha and Andrei worked for the KGB as the research and development scientist that's how they met Aija. While he was going through Andrei's things. The front door was opened.

Nikolai ducked and hid behind the couch in the living room. A young woman entered the house fearful at first. She checked the whole house before slumping on the couch and she cried inconsolably. She fell asleep and Nikolai got out behind the couch and was about to leave. He looked if he can see if he recognized the young lady. He opened her bag she had left on the table. He took her wallet and was about to open and take her ID out when the door suddenly opened and a man stood at the door looking at Nikolai. The voice of the man at the door startled him.

"Who are you? What are doing with that purse? Do you know Faye?"

Faye woke up after hearing the commotion.

Nikolai woke up with a heavy head and a broken jaw. His left side was swollen.

He realized that he was on the couch where the young lady was sleeping earlier on. The lady came in together with Bogdan her boyfriend.

"Who are you? What are you doing with my papa's photo?

"Your papa? Which one of the two is your papa?"

"What do you mean? Viktovha of course."

"You are Viktovha's daughter. The autopsy report was written that he had no kids."

"You listen to everyone and believe everything. That's your problem. What are you doing here anywhere?"

"Honestly I was asking myself the same question. I went to see the Vice President a few days ago, but I found out that she was dead."

"I know that's why we just returned today from hiding."

"Are you Andrei's son or something? What are you doing? Back from hiding as well, right?"

"No. I am a reporter I was investigating the death of Viktovha. I think he was set up. I think he told the security guards that he was her partner and they shot him on the spot. But what he actually meant was that they were lovers."

"I know she ruined my life too. She destroyed my family. She betrayed my father but Gezzy fixed her."

"What do you mean?"

"I can't believe that some people can be so cruel. She sent a hitman to shoot us down. Nearly a year now on the run. Then came the car chase. I shot one of the assassins before the other one died in car flames. But it was too late for Gezzy. I didn't know. He was shot and had lost a lot of blood. The next thing, he had a gun in his mouth and blew his brains out. He told me before he died that this was for the Vice President I knew what he meant."

"How is that so?"

"My papa; Viktovha the great, made a formula and because he was blinded by love, he gave the formula to the Vice President. They were lovers before and he was hooked on her. He sacrificed himself to save me. After she had sent a hitman after us Andrei. I mean Gezzy recreated the formula and gave himself the jabs. The day he died a few days ago, is the same day I heard that the Vice President died.

Nikolai took his bag and started looking at his notes.

"Roughly what time did Gezzy killed himself?"

"Let's see, around eight o'clock in the morning."

"So, in America, eight hours' difference, that means around four o'clock in the afternoon. Let's see. Where was I, around that time?"

Nikolai flipped through his notes as Faye looked on.

"Oh, yes. I was at the bank. Oh, my God," shouted Nikolai.

"The bank manager, the time I passed there he was dead. He shot himself. He looked like he had put a gun in his mouth and blew his brains out. But I checked there was no gun. I looked everywhere."

"You are scaring me now. What are you implying?" Nikolai paced in the living room for a while.

"I think I have to go. I must phone my boss. I will come and see you and talk to you if you are interested."

Nikolai took his stuff and left.

This was going to be the news headline of the year. He knew that something was just not right. He drove like a rally driver going back to the house in the countryside that belonged to the Vice President. He arrived there hoping to see her there. If she was still alive and in hiding the only place she could be, was this country house in Russia far away from the media and the city life and all the complaints about the jabs' side effects and all the lawsuits?

He arrived and went into the house and waited. He went to check in the basement and looked for any clues. He opened the big freezer downstairs. The first one was packed with fresh or still in date reindeer meat. He smiled. So, at one point she is planning to come here. He opened the second freezer.

He jumped in shock. There were two bodies in the fridge. One of a man and the other one's of a woman. They had clothes. He looked and discovered that their ID's were frozen with them.

Frantically all night he worked hard to defrost the deep freezer.

CHAPTER THIRTEEN

Faye stayed with her boyfriend Bogdan for some days before he went back to work, in Moscow. He had his own apartment in the city where they were staying together.

Even though the papers were saying that the Vice President had died. There was always a nagging feeling in her mind that what if she was still alive? The fact that Nikolai mentioned the bank manager dying the same way as Gezzy gave her sleepless nights.

She had thought that Gezzy had injected the same formula as the Vice President. So, it seems that the Vice President was still alive. Somehow maybe she had recreated another same formula and gave it to this bank manager. But that was just speculation.

Out of curiosity, she researched about this bank and this manager.

She couldn't believe the link. The bank was owned by the Vice President. It is claimed that the President's sample and money were stolen just a few days before both managers were found dead. She realized that the Vice President was cleverer than she had thought. She had made other similar formulas identical to hers and somehow, she must have escaped unless she had died too.

She checked reports about the Vice President's death. She was convinced that she had died. The next day she took her stuff from Andrei's place and went to her papa's house.

A gorgeous well-dressed woman boarded the plane wearing sunglasses, a wool floppy hat, and a gorgeous dress. She looked a million dollars. She had a veil covering her head too.

Halfway in the plane, she fell asleep and somehow the veil flipped to one side revealing half her face. The air hostess approached her and looked at her. She was asleep. So, she went to the office on the plane.

"Surely I thought that woman in seat seven was very familiar. Surely, I have seen her somewhere before. At one point, I thought that she was the Vice President of the United States of America.

"Flying in economy class what happened to air force one?"

"OK, you don't believe me. Come and see."

The two Latvian, air hostesses, approached the woman, but she was wide awake reading a magazine and her face covered. The air hostess passed-by and later returned to their office.

"She doesn't look like the Vice President. Maybe similar that's all."

"If you don't believe me, wait, I will bring up the passenger list."

The air hostess opened the passenger list on the computer.

"Here we go. Seat number seven window. Name is Elena."

The air hostess sat down confused that it wasn't her.

"See I told you it was not her."

Faye depressed about all this and a bit afraid arrived at her papa's house. She entered her bedroom and slept.

The following morning, she woke up to find a woman sitting in a chair in her bedroom.

Shocked and frightened she got up and tried to escape. She came face to face with the Vice President.

"I thought that you were dead? What are you doing here? What do you want? You cleaned up all my family you killed my papa why? You, spineless devil.

He loved you. Why you betrayed him? He gave you what you wanted. Why kill him? Why kill Gezzy too? Now you want to kill me. Where is my mum? I can't find her. Do you have something to do with this? I will kill you, myself."

The Vice President remained seated for some time before she stood up and walked toward Faye.

"Did you finished talking? I thought you were dead too. You betrayed me just like your father did. I loved him too, but he complained every day; I want a baby, I want a baby that drove me nuts. I wanted a baby too. I was so happy when I was with your father. I really wanted a baby too but somehow; I could not fall pregnant. We fought most of the time. I ended up marrying this man just for money and power. So, don't talk to me about betrayal. Viktovha drove me away with his complaining. Gezzy was bad as him too. He thought that he can give me away like an asset. Whenever his friend pretended to be stressed up. He will come and say, Aija my dear can you keep my friend company. That was worse. I felt cheap. You stand there and defend him. You must be out of your mind. He is as bad. I should have killed both a long time ago. One day they will learn to respect women. So, are you just going to stand there or what?"

Faye felt a huge block moving inside her heart she picked whatever she can and threw at Aija the Vice

President.

She jumped on her and the two women started fighting. At first, Aija did not hit her, she just received punches.

"So, you have revenged are you happy now? Can I go now? I have a plane to catch? I send you money. Here is another check. I feel like you are my daughter. Just because I loved your father I will spare your life and forever maintain peace. OK? I have enough blood on my hands. I am going."

Aija turned, about to live when Faye jumped on her back and strangled her from the back. The two women fell on the floor.

"Listen I don't want to kill you let me go."

"Say that to my papa. Say that to uncle Andrei. I think it's fitting to tell you also to say that to my mum."

"So, you want to die, you too? OK. I killed your father. I set him up. I killed Gezzy too. I killed your mother and I am going to kill you too."

Faye hysterically upon hearing about her mum she jumped on the Vice President. The two women struggled. The Vice President beat up Faye for the first time.

"Listen I am going. Like I said I have a plane to catch."

"Why my mother?"

Faye sat on the floor sobbing.

"Okay, you want to know why? I will tell you."

"Me and your father at one point we were about to get together. I was about to leave my job as a politician for your father. We had a good time. I was going to accept to marry him. He proposed to me before I had a chance to answer him guess who turned up? Your mother. Hey, hey, I can have kids. I can't say the same about some of you. That cheeky whore ruined my life. She told Viktovha that she was pregnant the day he proposed to me. I was going to marry him."

"So why kill my father and my mother and his best friend. It doesn't make any sense. You are a snake that kills for fun. Are you not?"

"You listen to me. I deserve to kill all. Your father asked me to set him up. He asked me to help him get killed."

"You lying coward. You kill for fun. Why would my father want to get himself killed? Is it because of this money? You! I going to kill you myself. You make me angry by lying."

The Vice President sat down on the chair in the room and took a deep breath.

"I loved Viktovha. I thought he was happy when one day he came to my office. He begged me to take care of you. I thought that he was still hooked on me. It was flattering, but I found that…"

The Vice President did not finish talking. She wiped tears from her face.

"Yes. Go on what did he tell you?"

"He said he was gutted that, that day he proposed I did not tell him my reply or expressed how I felt about his proposal."

"Why was that important after years? See, why I am saying that you are lying. He had mum and me why would he take his life because of you? You refused him several times, so?"

"I told your father the truth that I was going to say yes but your mother ruined everything for me."

"Maybe I have to get a gun and shoot you right now. You ruined my mother's life stop upsetting me with lies."

Faye looked for her bag and got a gun out. Shaking, she checked the magazine to see if the gun had bullets. She cried uncontrollably. She was shaking, and she pointed the gun at the Vice President.

Surprisingly the Vice President remained seated without expressing any panic.

"Are you going to let me finish first or what?"

"Just be careful what you say to me. I can't accept any silly games right now. You ruined my life and my family's life, so you deserve to die. I swear, if you lie one more time, I will smoke you like a dog."

"Your father came home and found your mother with his best friend."

"So, he told me about that. In fact, my mother went out with Gezzy first."

"Yes. That's when it. Started. The doubts about the pregnancy and everything. He started drinking not because of me like what everyone says, no. He found out that you were not his daughter."

A bullet was fired nearly missing the Vice President. Shaking and sobbing, Faye aimed the gun again at the Vice President.

"That's a warning. Keep lying and see. I swear by my mum I will smoke you today. Keep lying to me."

"He started drinking because your mother betrayed him. That day I was going to agree to marry Viktovha, your mother interrupted us before I said yes. She told him in front of me that he had got her pregnant. On hearing this I refused to marry your father only because of your mother. I left the country. I cried for months. After you were born, he told me he doubted that you were his.

Another bullet sends the Vice President ducking. Faye cried inconsolably.

"I told him that he was lying. I promised to marry him only if he can prove that you were not his daughter. So, I arranged the tests."

The Vice President paused and looked down.

Faye cried and sat down this time. She sat on the bed she holds the gun in her hands and put it on her forehead looking down. She raised her head and looked at the Vice President.

"So, what did you find out?" asked Faye.

"The day Viktovha came for the results of the test, before I told him, your mother out of the blues entered my office carrying you. I remember the first time I saw you. I felt like crying. I wished that you were my own. I hold you in my arms and I must confess. I have never seen Viktovha so happy."

"What were the results did you tell him."

"I told him that you were his. I didn't want to break such bonding. It was years later that he found out. You fall sick, and the doctors requested your father's blood. They refused his blood. He had suspected it, so he went and send Gezzy to donate blood."

"What are you saying? Are you saying that Viktovha is not my father?"

Faye looked confused. Her world was falling apart.

"Correct, look at this."

She took the results reports and looked at it. True Viktovha was not her father.

"That does not matter. I will kill you. Where is my mother? What did you do with my mother?"

"She was very upset. She came to my home in the countryside. She was drunk. She was angry she accused me of ruining her life because Viktovha found out that you were not his daughter. She fell by accident and died. I didn't know what to do. I live miles away I had no car those days. I called for help, but it was too late. She died at home.

Faye pointed the gun at the Vice President who stood up this time.

"Come on shoot me. I deserve to die. Shoot me, you coward. Just like your father. Shoot now or I will shoot you myself."

A gunshot sound rocketed in the whole house.

Nikolai in the morning checked the deep freezer and found that the ice on the bodies had melted. He looked at the corpse of the woman first and checked for ID. She had ID in her jacket.

He searched the pockets of the man he had ID too.

He sits down and took his laptop.

"Roy Fenrick and a one Magda Danske."

Whispered, Nikolai, reading the IDs.

After researching he discovered that it was the Senator. Senator Roy. The other lady had no idea who she was, but he got an address. He jumped into the car and drove as fast as he can.

He arrived outside the house and quickly entered the house.

"Ah no!"

Later.

Nikolai is holding Faye in her hands she had shot herself. She is dead. Gunshot wound in her head. A gun is next to her. While holding Faye in his hands he saw three-gun shells. He looked at her only one bullet wound. He stood up and looked around. He checked the walls and found two bullets lodged in the walls. He walked back to the bed and saw a paper. He picked it up. It's a birth certificate and a paternity test. He knew that the Vice President was there. He took the gun and left the house, going back to the country house that belonged to the Vice President.

Nikolai nears the yard of the property and a bullet smashed the windscreen of his car and the car veered before smashing on the nearby tree. Blood is coming out of Nikolai's forehead. The Vice President walked to the car and looked through the side window. A man walked toward her carrying a rifle.

"Who is he?"

"He is; 'have we met before', he just can't give up. I told him to back off. He knew I was alive. I met him at my office building. Did you send our boys already to his boss?"

"On their way as we speak."

"Ok let's go and clean the mess in the house before I go."

A smartly dressed woman entered a private jet and sits in the lounge suite. The pilot announced that the plane was going to take off soon. An air hostess came in and looked at the woman. "Do you want anything to drink, madam?"

The woman shook her head.

The jet plane flew for some time and the woman started dozing off.

The Vice President is outside Viktovha's place. She entered the house straight to a bedroom. She saw a lady sleeping like a baby. She sat down and cried. The lady is sleeping like there is no tomorrow.

She opened her bag and took out a checkbook. She wrote a check and left the check on the chair. She got up and was about to leave. She opened her bag and took out a paper, she read the paper before putting it back. She sat down. After some time, the lady woke up. They talked for some time. In the end, the lady aimed a gun at her. She reached inside the bag. The next thing she remembered is working on the floor.

She sat down and saw a lady lying in a pool of blood. She crawled toward her and when she arrived near her, she sat next to the lady. She cried inconsolably

"You coward! You coward! Why didn't you shoot me? I was sure you were going to shoot me. You are like a daughter to me. Just like your father, a coward. I love you. I tried to make things right, look what you've done. More blood on my hands, now even the Gods will not forgive me."

The Vice President slept next to the dead lady and hugged her all night.

A man slides the curtain in a private jet and stood looking at a sleeping woman in the plane.

"Mother what can I get you?"

The woman woke up and looked outside. She saw clouds through the small jet window. She looked at the man standing in front of her.

"A glass of wine and an orange juice."

The man is well-dressed up. He walked toward the refrigerator in the plane and opened the door. He looked in the fridge for the orange juice. After moving bottles around he found the juice. He was about to close the fridge door when he noticed cubed glass boxes with electrodes attached to them. Inside the glass, boxes are human organs.

He looked scared and quickly closed the door.

He walked into the Vice President's suite of the jet

plane.

"Where is my wine? You just brought orange juice for your wife what about my wine?"

"Sammy, why can't you listen to your mother. Even his child will be stubborn like him. Sorry, Mrs. Vice President, but your son sometimes makes me want to slap his face." said Nancy.

"Nancy my daughter-in-law calls me Aija I don't think

I want to be the Vice President anymore."

"Whose glass boxes, are they?"

The Vice President looked at her son, Sammy.

"Senator Roy's?"

"Why? I thought his double died…"

The Vice President looked outside the window of the jet plane first before looking at Nancy who was heavily pregnant and touched her big belly.

"The Senator was my double."

"Senator Roy, your death partner?"

Mother and son exchanged a quick glance.

A man walked into a country house and into the basement. He saw two corpses on the floor. He carried the corpse of Senator Roy and placed it in the deep freezer. He was shocked by his weight. He looked inside his shirt. He had no organs inside all removed. He carried the corpse of the women and it felt heavy. He placed the corpse in the freezer and closed it. He walked outside the house to a car slumped on a tree. He looked inside and searched the pockets of the dead man in the car.

"Nikolai a news reporter, huh? What are you going to report now that you are dead?" said the man before carrying the body of Nikolai into the house and straight into the other deep freezer.

In the jet plane, Sammy walked into the refrigerated cargo area of the jet plane and opened the heavy doors. He looked like he had seen a ghost. The cargo compartment was full of human organs in glass cubes with electrodes attached to them.

Later, Sammy, his wife Nancy and the Vice President Aija are watching the news.

"Just in. The director of the news channel has been found dead today. His death is not being treated as suspicious."

Sammy flicked to another news channel.

"The Just-jabs and the Breathbank companies formerly owned by the Vice President Aija have been sold to a Russian billionaire but the government still has some shares in the company and some vested interests. Lizzy reporting for Breathbank news."

The jet plane disappeared into the clouds.

****

THE END

ABOUT ELINA SALAJEVA

I am a young author as well as a motivational speaker and have written several books.

The Girl with The Tiger Tattoo and The Magnificent Six

Brexit: Aftermath. What Is the Way Forward?

The Vice President

The Vice President: The Rise of The Word-Command Killer. The Independent Adjudicator

Chase Your Dreams Never Give Up

The Vice President: Foreign Frights. The $50 000 Club

Adventures of Neo and Joe

Fight for Honor

Do You Fancy A $25 000 Publishing Deal?

Where Are You, My Love?

The Vice President

Elina Salajeva

The Vice President

Elina Salajeva